SIR HENRY'S HAUNTED TALES

THE MAKER

The character Sir Henry was born out of my love for Halloween. Growing up, I had large elaborate yard displays for Halloween, which created a fondness for me from an early age for the holiday. The older I got, the more I reflected on why I loved it so much and what made it special to me.

There was always something so magical about the October season and Halloween night. My mom would read me many Halloween books as a child, even outside of the month of October. She would read them over and over again just because I loved them so much. My father would also tell me multiple stories about Halloween monsters and villains, but I remember he would place me in the center of them as the hero. The stories were always so descriptive and created vivid images that lived on in my memory. They had great suspense and heart, but there was also an element of realism to them that made them so believable. I think all of these factors played into me appreciating the holiday just a little more than the average Trick or Treater.

I never wore a store-bought Halloween costume. They were never original enough for me. I always had to be creating something new. Once I was old enough to start creating my own displays, I found an even bigger outlet for my creativity and my love for the holiday. Each year the display grew bigger, and so did the crowds.

One Halloween while brainstorming a potential character, I had a vision of a dapper skeleton wearing a top hat and bow tie. The image stuck with me and I decided to bring it to life. After putting together a top hat, a three piece suit, a purple bow tie, and skeleton mask, even though I didn't know it at the time, the legend of Sir Henry was born. Only later once I started my own haunted attraction and was looking for an icon character for it would I come back to this character. He was the perfect symbol for Halloween. The name Sir Henry came from the street I grew up on where all of my childhood Halloween memories were made.

Sir Henry is a trickster. Sure, a skeleton is classic Halloween, but he also has a regalness that the holiday carries. He is a hero, just like the one that my dad made me in all of those stories many years ago. I never envisioned him as a villain - Halloween has plenty of those. He is an anti-hero. The audience can root for and relate to him, both in tragedy and triumph.

The way my beloved Sir Henry and related characters have been brought to life is unreal. To me, it shows how relatable this universe is. I was nervous about handing over my beloved characters to someone to write about. I could not have asked for anyone better to do it.

The attention to detail and care that has been taken is second to none. A huge thank you to Amanda Rosenblatt and Brad Acevedo for that! I know that when you read this book, a whole new world will be opened up and a plethora of new Halloween characters will find a special place in your heart. I hope it sparks your imagination and love for Halloween just like my dad did for me all those years ago telling me Halloween bedtime stories. -Zach Glaros

THE AUTHOR

Ever since I was a little girl, Halloween was one of the most important days of the year for me. As an adult, when my husband and I moved cross-country to Tampa Bay from San Diego, we scoped out seasonal activities we wanted to do, and Halloween (IE September & October) is a must. Sir Henry's was 100% on the radar, which we knew at the time as the I-Four Fear Park.

The first time my husband and I went to Sir Henry's in October of 2019, we were blown away. The storytelling was unforgettable. Fresh memories of characters wandering the center of the grounds interacting with guests, an amazing centerpiece with lights that synced up with music, and the classic film "Psycho" playing on a projector. What a treasure.

Then, 2020 happened. We were able to attend the Sir Henry's Valentines Day horror event in February, and just weeks later, the world changed due to COVID-19. Despite a dark year of loss and cancelled events due to this pandemic, Sir Henry's put on a safe Fall event that was as amazing as ever. Sure, we wore masks and stood six feet apart, but for a few hours, it felt like normal life. The soul of Halloween was still thriving.

I was so thrilled that Zach trusted his characters and this world to my care. I thank him for having this project to work on. I also thank my husband, the marvelous horror writer Brad Acevedo, for crafting two chapters (the stories of Pyrum and Kane are his creation) and for his encouragement. To the readers, thanks for grabbing this book! See you in the fog. -*Amanda Rosenblatt*

ABOUT "SIR HENRY'S HAUNTED TRAIL"

Plant City is a lovely town in Central Florida. Known as the winter strawberry capital of the world, most would otherwise overlook it as merely a pitstop on your way either to Orlando or Tampa. But just off of Interstate 4, in the woods lies an amazing secret world.

Sir Henry's Haunted Trail is a horror-themed attraction that has been in operation since 2014. With multiple houses, immersive characters, and a high-quality experience, it attracts year-round horror fanatics and Halloween time spook-seekers alike.

Ground-breaking not only for its characters and set pieces, Sir Henry's is also known for its diverse offerings. In the winter around Christmastime, the property transforms into a family-friendly attraction to celebrate the joyous season. When Valentine's Day comes around, hardcore haunt fans can enjoy an off-season event with a horrifying romantic twist.

The best part about Sir Henry's is the altruistic background it holds. Other than regularly donating proceeds to various charities, many of the stories behind the houses or walk-through trails often represent various Biblical tales. Many appreciate that the haunt shows you can have a religious background while also enjoying the horror genre without judgement.

Serious haunt seekers should certainly schedule to put Plant City on their maps during Fall to experience this iconic attraction. Sir Henry eagerly awaits your RSVP.

PROLOGUE
Sir Henry

October 31st, 1929.

It is a chilly but clear afternoon. A young man in a dapper suit exits his Model A Ford. He wears a black lounge coat, a crushed velvet undershirt, dress shoes, a bowtie, and a black top hat. Typical formal attire for most men of this day and age, but this gentleman has unique accents of amethyst purple, compliments of his bowtie and top hat band.

Such a bright shade was never his first choice, but it was her favorite color.

He steps over fresh cut grass, walking slowly but with a purpose. He holds white roses, and shortly reaches his destination. He removes his hat in respect.

"Darling, how I wish you were here," he whispers. He looks upon the newly installed gravestone of a woman who has passed too soon. The dirt of her grave is still fresh, as the burial was just this past week.

A Joyful Light, Extinguished.

A simple inscription on the slab of granite. No name or dates. The marker of a final resting place for his Bride. Her sudden and mysterious death, which took place only days ago, left the young man shaken in the aftermath of the morbid event.

He kneels slightly, placing the flowers on the ground in front of the headstone. He lifts his left hand and presses it against the rock. As cold as her flesh was when he identified the body at the police station. Expression blank, jaw slack.

He shakes his head of the dark memory, his stark blue eyes filling with tears. He gazes at his Bride's grave for a moment longer. A cold breeze caresses his face as the sun begins to set.

The mourner walks back to his car to prepare himself for the long ride home. As he settles into his seat with the door shut, his mind is numb yet it runs wild with ideas all at once.

His new daily thoughts are enveloped by what caused her demise. The police had gathered, rather hastily, that she died of a heart attack, which was a new medical terminology that had premiered in the past decade. Boggy Meadow was a small town, so they had no medical examiners like a big city would have. Especially with the Great Depression casting a dark shadow across America, it was easy to blame a lack of resources on not properly investigating what he felt was foul play.

When someone met their end in this town, you dealt with only the Schwartz Funeral Home, if you were lucky. That was if someone passed away peacefully in their sleep or from an illness you knew of. Those were instances you come to expect.

But when the police come up your driveway in the middle of the day to say that your young

Bride was found dead in an alley near the community market? You never expect that.

There were many things that led the man to believe it was not a biological factor that was her undoing. Bruises on her wrists and no prior history of health problems. Plus, there was the matter of the town not being enthusiastic about the man, his Bride and their presence here at all. Why wouldn't he suspect corruption on some level?

Time spent driving has passed, and the man hits the brake pedal. He leaves the car running and honks his horn twice. A person eventually appears and unlocks the gate, rolling it open so the vehicle may enter. He drives underneath a wooden archway that reads "Sir Henry's Carnival of Freaks."

He makes his way up the driveway and parks. It is now a twilight blue outside and the air has become colder. He feels the biting wind on his cheeks as he fully exits the car interior. His home is at the rear of his fair ground, overlooking his macabre creation.

"How did it turn out?"

He turns to Galinda, the bearded lady, one of his surrogate family members and friends at the fair. He smiles half-heartedly, tears once again making his eyes warm. "It's a beautiful headstone, fitting for her sense of minimalism, really," he utters softly.

She offers a comforting hand on his shoulder, squeezes slightly, and then removes it to scratch the stubble on her right cheek. "Did I mention it's weird we aren't open on Halloween? I hate to complain - just want us to open back up so I can clean this itchy mess."

He shrugs. "I imagine we will soon. I just need more time, but not to worry. You know this is your home. Enjoy the time off." He turns and heads up the path to his modest two story home. An extinguished Jack-o-lantern sits on the ground near the door. Galinda looks upon him with concern, but she eventually turns and heads back to her quarters.

Sir Henry's was known as a refuge for the unaccepted. The outcasts and freaks. If they were willing to be self-deprecating towards the things that made them unique and could be coached to have showmanship, they received food, shelter, and a makeshift family in return.

Galinda, for instance, had hypertrichosis, which made her an incredible bearded lady. What society saw as problems, Sir Henry's saw as gifts.

The fairgrounds held a decent sized farm, a small patch of field where corn grew, and a large barn where animals occupied the bottom floor. The top level was renovated to be comfortable living quarters for the stars of his show. Everyone had their own small room with a bed, a chair, a dresser, and a window.

While many traveled far and wide to see his fairgrounds, the townsfolk were not so thrilled. Their small infrastructure was not built for the influx of tourism, but they also did not want to be known as Freak Town, as the city council called it. Even with the money that the show brought in during such financially trying times, it was not enough good will, it seemed.

Time and time again, they have been told to pack it up and head out. But this was home, not a traveling circus. Sir Henry's was not going anywhere, even though they called him a ghoul, a subvert, and a shyster. All of which were untrue and disheartened him, but he continued on.

The animosity that the town held for the carnival coupled with the recent, tragic loss of the Bride caused a good portion of the freaks to part ways after the funeral was over. While he was both the spine and brain of this place, she was the heart. Some could not bear to be here any longer without her warm spirit. Her cheerful smile as she repaired rips in their costumes. The smell of her fresh baked pies wafting through the air from the kitchen windowsill. All gone.

The man makes his way up the stairs of his empty home. These walls were supposed to be filled with the joyous sounds of children. Another sad thought crowding his weary mind.

He carefully takes off his suit piece by piece, organizing it in a flat-lay on the bed. He walks over to his wardrobe to grab a garment bag and neatly gathers the suit into it. The last bit was his top hat, which he looks upon with mixed emotions. This was his showman's hat, but the Bride loved it on him and encouraged him to wear it while out and about. *Keep your head up*, she would say, *or else your crown will tip over.*

He was not sure when he would be ready to go on with the show again, but he knew for her, he could not give up. He hangs up the garment bag on a clothes rack in the room, the hat being the final garnish at the top. He slips on his nighttime robe and crawls into bed, praying for the comforting haze of sleep to bring his mental state elsewhere.

****

Screams. Heat. Smoke. "Help!"

He wakes from a dark, dreamless slumber. He jolts upright, turns his head left to right to try and evaluate his surroundings. The clock reads 11:32 PM.

He pushes himself out of bed, pure adrenaline taking over. He goes to the window and opens it, smoke creeping into his bedroom. He turns and witnesses that across the field, the barn, the quarters are on fire.

"Galinda!" He hollers for his longtime friend. She comes into view, her clothes and hair singed. "The place was set on fire! Someone had to have done it. No one here is dumb enough to break the 'no candles' rule. We live in a damn barn!" She takes a moment to gather her breath. "I'm going to get as many out as I can. Go get the fire brigade!"

He gasps, overlooking the scene. It looks as if a few made it out so far and were pumping water from the well into a bucket to help put the fire out. He hoped his cows and chickens were able to run away into the woods.

He did not want the fire getting to his house or to any of the exhibits, so he had to act fast. He runs over to the telephone in the hallway, shakily using the rotary to dial the town's emergency services, but it rings without answer. He grunts angrily and throws the receiver down, fumbling back over to the window.

He scans over the scene and sees a dark figure skulking around in the bushes near the wooden archway. They push the fence open and escape. Tears of rage slip down Sir Henry's face and he flies quickly down the stairs. He grabs his car keys, exiting his front door and hastily getting in the vehicle. He sees Galinda in the rear view mirror waving her arms at him, but he looks ahead to the road.

He starts the car, peeling off into the night. He scans the road furiously, the smoke from the barn hovering in the cold air around the property. "Where are you?!" He yells helplessly, wanting to catch sight of this menace. He suddenly hits a large rock in the unpaved road, causing him to lose stability of the car. He gasps and hits the brakes, but he is terrified to discover that they had been cut.

His car continues to barrel down the road, refusing to slow. He tries to stop the car by downshifting into lower gears while keeping his foot off the gas pedal, but his initial speed made the effort futile. With a tree coming up fast at a fork in the road, he turns the wheel as quickly to the left as possible, hoping it would help the car to stop, or at least hit the tree on the passenger side. The plan backfires, his current momentum causing the car to spin in a 360 degree direction. With a loud metallic crunching noise and the shattering of glass echoing in the quiet night, the driver side directly smashes against the heavy trunk of the tree.

The sudden quantity of pain was too much. He was not concerned with what in his body was broken and punctured. The copper taste of blood pouring from his mouth was quickly fading away. His mind is no longer plagued with how he would make it another day without his Bride.

He looks up at the clear night sky, feels the cold breeze on his face, and he closes his mortal eyes for the last time.

***

The Month of September, 1932.

America is still in the midst of the Great Depression. Many struggle to survive, and those with money are very protective of it.

Mr. Barloc, a young Millionaire, is one of the lucky survivors. Right after finishing business school, he came into a small fortune after his father's death in 1926. From this inheritance, he was able to grow his money from smart investments. While he is a man of mathematics and finances, he holds an interesting secret.

Ever since he was a little boy, he has been plagued with hyper-realistic dreams. Clairvoyant visions when he slept. Dreams of bullies chasing him down and beating him to death, or falling into an open manhole were just some graphic visions he has woken from in a cold sweat quite a few times.

Though detailed and terrifying, instead of ignoring the dreams, he used them as study materials to sidestep tragedy. In the early mornings as a boy, he would walk the paths projected mentally to him in which bullies chased him. This enabled him to find successful hiding places when the pursuits actually occurred. Years later while in town to fetch a prescription for his father, he felt an eerie sense of deja vu when he came across an open, unattended sewer hatch.

As he became an adult, the dreams were less frequent, but still valuable. The visions never led him to financial glory, as that was more to the credit of his economic knowledge. Luckily, frequent nightmares of standing outside his foreclosed townhouse in the Summer of 1929 prompted him to pull all of his stocks from the Market. After about a week of wondering if he had made a mistake, the Great Depression reared its head.

While he was not in as prosperous a position as he was before this economic crash, he made conversative choices in order to survive. After watching his father die slowly of cancer years prior, he was inspired to spend time researching labs and companies who could make a difference for these victims and investing in them.

Years went by without the dreams occurring. It was a relatively peaceful existence. The only exception was one random night in October of 1929, he recalled waking up in a fright from a dream where he was in a car crash. The vision didn't make much sense to him though, as he did not own a Ford and the crash seemed to be in the middle of nowhere, while he lived in a metropolitan city. He paid attention if the dream happened again, but it did not, so he moved on.

After years of silent slumber, in the Fall of 1932, they came back with a vengeance. Blurry visions of being trapped in an enclosed, dark space. A grave. Digging with a shovel. He woke up from these dreams each time, crazed and confused. Usually, they were easy to decipher, but he couldn't make heads or tails of what this all meant.

Days into this mental torture of not being able to sleep through the night, he decides to do some tidying up. In the midst of organizing his bedroom closet, he comes across an old box of belongings labeled CHILDHOOD MEMORIES. He places the box on a chair next to his bed and opens the lid. After shuffling through some photos, his hands come across a wrinkled piece of paper.

Come one, come all, to Sir Henry's Carnival of Freaks!

A flyer yellowed with age. Memories came flooding back to him, but he merely smiles and places it back into the box. Once he was satisfied with his cleaning activities, he retired to bed to try once more to sleep.

The dream that follows is crystal clear. More detailed than ever. He is standing before a statue of Sir Henry, the fairgrounds abandoned. He can smell the wet grass and hear crickets chirp. Whispers, at first quiet, were now deafening. He blinks to try and snap out of it, and when his eyes open, the ground is littered with glowing Jack-o-lanterns.

Dig. Dig. Dig. DIG. DIG. DIG!

He wakes, gasping for air. Throwing himself out of bed, he goes to his closet, grabs the box of memories he found earlier, tosses the lid aside, and rifles furiously through the items. With enough force to elicit papercuts, he finally locates what he needed. His blood drips upon the Sir Henry's flyer, as he circles the address on it with a nearby pen. It is still far too early to do anything about this, so he spends more time researching medical books to calm his nerves until the sun comes up.

A few hours later, tired but determined, he calls his real estate agent and asks if this property, some random address seemingly in the middle of nowhere, is for sale. Though incredulous of his spontaneous request, the realtor was able to collect the information needed within a business day.

"So the property has been vacant for a few years, since the owner died. There's a large house of decent structure, all of the original belongings still in it, and a generous portion of land. A burnt down husk of a barn is still on the property, a rotten field of corn, and here's the kicker. There's a centerpiece statue of some circus fella in a top hat right in the middle. Sounds like a damn mess, to me!"

I have no patience for this tedious man, Mr. Barloc thinks to himself. "Right. And is it for sale?"

"The land is definitely affordable and would make a lovely country getaway, or a bed and breakfast, I'm sure. The listing even states if you buy the land, the Mayor's office will have a local construction crew come down and clear out the existing structures for you. That's the first I've ever heard of anything like that! Country folk sure are odd."

He sure is a chatty bastard. "I don't just want the land, though. I want the house and anything that remains on the property."

There is silence on the other end, then uproarious laughter. "Well hey pal, a commission is a commission. If you want it, I'll make arrangements."

***

The Month of October, 1932.

After hours on the road, his Cadillac V-16 having hit every bump along the way and his roadmap creased from overuse, Mr. Barloc is finally able to recognize his surroundings. It was amazing what subconsciously came back to him. He drives further until he reaches a fork in the road, passing a stately tree with a large gash on the side of it. He eventually is met with the gate.

He had a hard time believing it, but it was still here. The late afternoon sun shines upon the archway. He regards a steel gate with a padlock chain keeping the curious world out. Above him, he notices that someone had previously torn off all the letters except the word FREAKS.

He hits the brake, leaves the engine running and walks around the side of his vehicle. He unlatches his rear trunk and pulls out the bolt cutters that the realtor said he would need. After some effort, the corroded lock hits the ground with a thud. Mr. Barloc removes the chain and pulls the gate open as much as possible, as it was now rusted with age.

He slowly drives his car past the gate and up the driveway of the old house. After parking securely, he trudges across the overgrown grass to the gate, making sure to close it via a rickety latch. As he walks back to the house, he pauses to survey the statue in the middle of the grounds. A monument to Sir Henry and his fallen kingdom, tarnished by the elements, and a crow's nest situated on the crown of the top hat. He lets out a sigh.

"I don't know what you need from me, but I'll clean this place up until we figure it out," he mutters to the statue.

***

October 31st, 1932.

11:32 PM and not a soul for miles is awake. It is Halloween night, and it is a leap year.

Any Jack-o-lanterns on doorsteps to celebrate the holiday, or perhaps to ward off ancient spirits, have long since gone dark. The local cemetery is quiet and still in the cold night air. The silence is soon broken by haunting, wretched noises.
Gasping. Kicking against moist wood.
Mournful, confused cries for help. After bracing both hands and one foot against damp planks,

pushing in unison as the other foot stabilizes his weight, flimsy nails give way. A filthy, horrified man is able to escape from what would have been his grave.

He turns, catching his breath after escaping the darkness. He sees that he was buried in a cheap pine box, only shut with three nails, recognized by a simple wooden cross with no markings. A pauper's burial. There is a pile of fresh dirt by the grave. Was he just tossed into the ground without being covered by the Earth - a dignity every man has earned?

He further examines his surroundings. He cannot smell anything and despite however long he was buried, he does not feel hunger or thirst, but he concludes that this was likely due to shock. He stands shakily, rubbing as much dust as possible off his simple burial garb, not being able to see much due to the cover of night and still being disoriented.

He recognizes that he is situated towards the rear part of the cemetery and gathers himself. He walks with a limp over to a nearby tombstone as if drawn to it, letting out a sigh of relief when he finally sets his eyes upon it.

"Thank God you're still here," he says to the grave of his Bride, voice hoarse.

"S-Sir Henry?" He turns and sees another young man, a shovel in one hand and a dull lantern in the other. The color is drained from his face, eyes wide open.

"What is this? Who are you?" The other man gulps and finds his voice. "My name is Barloc, Mr. Barloc. I have much to tell you."

***

On the long car ride back to the fairgrounds, Mr. Barloc tells his exhumed passenger that years had gone by, about what had become of his business. Shortly after his accident, for which there was no funeral, the town's people ran the freaks away, locking the gates of the property and leaving it to fester in isolation.

Sir Henry asks if anyone made it out of the fire, and Mr. Barloc answers that the newspapers failed to cover the "shame" of what had transpired. He shares that in his research, the only information he tracked down was that Galinda had gone on to a position of fame as a performer for a traveling circus. "How did you know to find me, and that I would return?" Sir Henry asks.

Mr. Barloc thinks before choosing his words. "I have these, these dreams, I guess you could say. Visions that led me back out here. It's hard to explain. Usually, it's just dreams, but coming here, it's as if the abilities have awakened even more. I hear voices during the day now. It didn't happen until I was cleaning up your old belongings this afternoon and I came across an invoice from the local cemetery. Looking at the address at the top of the sheet, the voices started repeating the same word, over and over. DIG. I grabbed a shovel, drove out there, and found this grave I saw multiple times in my dreams. Your grave. I basically just removed the dirt over your coffin, but I never would have thought..."

Sir Henry nods, turning his gaze out the window and looking up at the stars. Upon arriving back, Mr. Barloc helps Sir Henry out of the car and back into the house. "You cleaned everything up nice, for it being abandoned so long," he utters, his voice ragged.
"Don't speak, you've been through a traumatic experience. Let's draw you a bath. I'll go find some of your old clothes."

They make their way into the master bathroom and Mr. Barloc turns on the faucet of the clawfoot tub. While the water runs, he leaves briefly and returns with both a burlap bag and a sleeping robe. He places both on a foot bench next to the bath, along with clean towels, and then shuts off the water. He doesn't miss a beat - the muscle memory of caring for his ill father years prior aiding him through his fatigue.

"Well, I need to get some rest. Since this is your house, I relinquish the master bedroom to you. See you in the morning."

Once alone, Sir Henry peels off the clothing he was buried in and places it in the sack. He braces himself and sinks into the warm soapy water. He feels a strange sensation - usually, a bath should feel soothing, but it feels foreign. He takes a cloth hanging on the side of the tub, and he scrubs the dirt and dust away. He gasps and feels panic as he uncovers the layers of filth that coated him for several years. He struggles to keep his voice down, as he does not want to scare his gracious rescuer.

His skin has an odd texture - a gray, almost mummified surface. Akin to leather. The flesh of his hands envelops his fingers almost to the point that they look like a skeleton's hand. There was no rotting, no sight of his veins or organs. He slaps himself repeatedly, willing himself to wake from this nightmare.

How could I still be alive? He concludes that neither he, nor Mr. Barloc, could see the extent of decomposition due to how dark it was outside and how dirty he was after his escape from the grave. He splashes water all over himself in a frenzy, scrubs at his arms, his shoulders, his chest, legs, neck, face. He pulls the plug out of the tub's drain and lets the muddied water circle down.

After covering himself with a towel, he limps cautiously to the mirror, bracing himself for what he would see. He looks back at a stranger in the mirror. A walking skeleton, barely an owner of any muscle to speak of. No lips, with his teeth on full display. His eyes, still a stark piercing blue, surrounded by sunken, black flesh.
He spends much time studying this new face, grieving what was and accepting what is. *I'm*

finally the ghoul they accused me of being, he thinks to himself in defeat.

He dresses himself with his sleeping robe and carries his lantern from the bathroom to his bedside table. He extinguishes the light and slowly climbs into bed. He did not want to sleep, as he had been buried for years, so instead, he let his mind race.

Why had he come back, but his Bride could not? Was there some greater purpose to his supernatural return? Was it a cruel mistake of the Heavens, or was this Hell?

Eventually, his decrepit body gives into exhaustion and against his will, he sleeps.

***

In the morning, a fog crawls over the ground and the sun refuses to appear. The cold wind whips furiously through the trees, with the smell of rain hanging in the air.

Mr. Barloc sits in a lounge chair near a roaring fire, reading one of many books he brought with him to pass the time. He hears creaks on the wooden floor, but they stop just outside of the room.

"Thank you for everything you have done," Sir Henry says, concealing himself.

Mr. Barloc puts down his book. "Of course. I cleaned my car out when the sun came up. Couldn't really stay asleep, I suppose. How are you feeling?"

Silence. "I am still confused by it all. I think you should leave. I can barely look at myself. To have someone I barely know who has done all he has for me to be frightened to death. I could not have that on my conscience."

Mr. Barloc looks around the corner, but his visitor refuses to make himself known. "You know, when I was a boy, I stuttered, which made me a target. Since I was always so alone, I found that I loved reading horror novels, anatomy books. I loved science and math. For all my differences, the other children did not understand me and they made that quite clear," he said, his voice somber.

"The one place I never felt judged was when we made the long pilgrimages out here a few times a year. To your freak show," Mr. Barloc said, struggling to allow the word "freak" to escape from his mouth. "No, you do not know me, but something greater than us caused our paths to cross. You unknowingly helped me through a difficult period of my life, and it is only fitting I return the favor."

After more silence, Sir Henry finally appears. He wears the same telltale suit he wore to visit his Bride's new tombstone years ago. His cane, which was once used for showmanship as part of his costume, was now quite handy in steadying his gait. The light from the crackling fire dances across his shriveled flesh, magnifying his shocking experience.

Mr. Barloc takes a deep breath, registering the sight, but he does not scream, gasp, or even flinch. He instead stands from his chair, and turns to grab an item from the fireplace mantle.

It is a brand new silk hatbox. He lifts the lid and brings it over. "I think the outcasts of the world deserve Sir Henry's return."

He feels many emotions stir about him as he retrieves his headgear. A mixture of hope, a lingering anger for what the townspeople have done to him, and gratitude towards his new companion.

"There is much work to be done," Sir Henry says, one bony hand lifting his signature hat atop his skull. "But the show must go on."

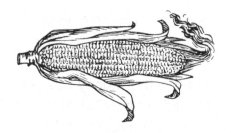

CHAPTER 1
The Harvester

Early Spring, 1933

Mr. Barloc wipes the sweat from his forehead with a rag, sticks it in his pocket, and continues to till the dirt. Already he and Sir Henry have made great efforts to resuscitate the property. Barloc has been able to run necessary errands and hire discreet contractors with cash while Sir Henry works behind the scenes, hidden from the daylight and away from prying eyes.

Sir Henry had no heirs or family to contact at the time of his death years prior, and the town just abandoned his property. This was fortunate for his unexpected resurrection, since the young showman did not trust banks. Along with Barloc's line of credit from the city, Sir Henry has been able to use the untouched money from the safe in his basement to fund these efforts.

It was a relief that this money was sealed from moisture and did not mold while stashed away over the years, but he had also purchased the best safe he could possibly find once the Great Depression had begun. There was however concern, as the money slowly dwindled away due to this project.

Fixing the barn, ordering livestock from the bordering county, supplies for farming, painting buildings, scheduling for monthly supply deliveries, and bringing out electricity linemen to make sure power could finally reach property. These efforts were expensive, but for Sir Henry, it was worth every penny after the devastation the fire had caused. He was thankful his house somehow survived that horrific night.

Sir Henry stands at the kitchen counter, watching Barloc grapple with the physical task from the window. He felt horrible he could not help, but they could not risk him being seen. There was also the issue of Sir Henry's physical state. How much harm could the hot sun do to him? Rain? Snow? It was obviously new territory to meander through. He knew for certain, however, that when it was time to reopen the property to the public, the night air would be most suitable. He has already been slowly easing himself back into the outside world under the cover of night.

For the past week, he would leave the house, the stars and moon keeping him company, and he would help physically however he could while Barloc slept. He had already replaced the letters on the archway, but the next task was a point of pride.

Two nights prior, he had asked Barloc to leave the materials out to revamp the centerpiece statue. He grabbed a ladder, gingerly moved the bird nest to a safe place, and began his work. The reflection of the rising sun shining against the newly restored metal after hours of hard work was his signal to get inside.

After savoring this warm memory, Sir Henry turns away from the window and walks to his study. There on the desk, he carefully unwraps a package that was delivered earlier. He unveils a stack of flyers.

Come one, come all - witness the Phantom of Sir Henry! Along with his menagerie of misfits, they seek their revenge on the judgmental living who have cast them out. Do you dare seek the horrors of the Otherside? Merely 25 cents for entry, and 10 cents per attraction!

Sir Henry chuckles. Barloc has talked him into this story twist. What better way to drum up business than a ghost story? During the Great Depression, folks amused themselves on the cheap by seeing horror movies, or they created their own haunted houses, as many could not afford candy to give out at Halloween. With this information, they brainstormed on what they called a year-round haunt. It was worth a try.

They made sure before any work on the land occurred that they nailed Sir Henry's coffin shut, covered the grave with dirt, and germinated the ground as hastily as possible. Such time had passed, many likely forgot the tales of that old abandoned freak show in the woods. If they had not, even better! Urban legends might help drive business.

With a newly acquired list of town halls, civic centers, dance halls, movie theaters, and rotary clubs within a 20 mile radius in hand, Sir

Henry pulls up a chair. He prepares a stack of envelopes, along with his quill pen and ink. The plan is to package up the flyers and send them out once work on the property is complete. This included locating performers for the show, but it was all in good time.

Meanwhile outside, Mr. Barloc is nearly done with his task. While they could hire an extra hand to get the corn patch revitalized, saving money in the process was crucial. That and after reading both a Farmers Almanac and an agriculture book, he felt slightly confident enough to do it himself.

He lifts his farming hoe and connects it to the ground, but he strikes something solid. He lets out a sigh, drops the hoe and kneels down. He grabs a nearby trowel to sift through the soil. He scrapes across what he thinks is a rock, digging his left hand into the ground to locate the foreign object.

He pulls out what looks like a tibia bone. He furrows his brow, trying to catch his breath from both physical exertion and the shock of this discovery.

***

It is evening, and Mr. Barloc lies in the guest room, begging his mind to give in to sleep. He is exhausted, but he is still shaken up from what he found while farming earlier. He did not tell Sir Henry about it yet - he skipped dinner and quietly ascended to his room, changing out of his dirty clothes.

Soon, he is granted sleep. In his slumber however, a disturbing dream finds him.

***

A little boy stands on the doorstep of a two story house. He overlooks a barn and a field of corn. He waves to an older man who is working in the field this morning.

The boy walks over to the field of maize, regarding one of the ears of corn as he glides his finger over the dry kernels. He feels joy.

"It is a blessing that the farm is finally flourishing," the boy says.

"Aye, especially with a horrible drought. It shows God has not forgotten us out here," An older woman says, who is a few rows of corn separate from her two family members.

The boy grabs a basket of picked corn that was placed on the grass beside the crops, grunting as he picks it up. He winces in pain, as he is still tender from the whupping he received days prior.

He has a brief flashback of asking his father why they have so much corn and why they don't try to sell it to their neighbors. A simple observation that cost a belt to his backside.

As the little boy struggles to carry the corn up the doorstep into his home, he hears a strange noise. It is similar to the call of a cow, which would not be odd to come across on a farm, but since they only had chickens on property, he carefully regards the sound.

He tries to locate the echoing noise. He puts down the basket and investigates, walking along the side of his house. He crouches near the basement window, hearing the noise again. He struggles, but eventually pushes the glass door open, carefully climbing down into the underbelly of the home. He uses a pile of chopped firewood to traverse backwards, reaches the ground and turns around to explore the mysterious noise.

There is a horrific stench in the basement, and he pinches two fingers over his nose to keep the smell out of his nostrils. All around are baskets of what looks like mulch or compost. There is a meat grinder in the corner with flies circling all around it.

He hears the moan again. He scans his surroundings, not sure what is where. He thinks to himself that the basement has been locked recently and he always pondered why. He feels dread creep over him.

He sees a box of papers near a desk. He grabs one, and in rough handwriting, it states *FRESH CORN - BROWN FAMILY FARM - COME TO THE GATE BETWEEN NOON AND 1. HAND DELIVERIES ONLY.*

He sees a large wooden chest in the corner. His heart races. The smell is stronger. He wills himself to place both hands on the lid of the chest, and he lifts. He screams.

A man is inside. All of his limbs are gone, but he is somehow still alive. He is pale from blood loss, festering in the enclosed box. Maggots eat at the necrotic flesh of this poor soul.

"P-please kill me."

Tears roll out of the boy's eyes and he gasps for air between terrified sobs. He turns and climbs out of the window, some of the firewood logs rolling away from the force of his escape.

He runs through the corn field in a panic. He does not know what to do or where to go. He comes across the older woman, who has a trowel and a bucket of the same mulch material from the basement. She is peeling flesh off of a bone. She meets her son's gaze- shame and fear in her glaring eyes.

"Mother?" He feels a hand on his shoulder spin him around forcefully. The older man towers over him. He looks at the boy, tears of anger glittering in the morning sun. "I am sorry, my son, but our family must survive."

The father is holding a scythe stained with dried blood. He wrenches it back around his shoulder, gripping the wooden handle with both hands, and swings it towards the small boy with force.

***

Barloc screams, jolting upright in bed. Huffing, sweaty and shaken up from the graphic nightmare. After collecting himself, he removes the covers and leaves the bedroom.

He makes his way downstairs and though it is late in the night, Sir Henry is still at work. Physically writing out addresses on envelopes and neatly folding adverts into them.

When Barloc sees the flyers on the desk, he feels a knot in stomach, recounting the hyper-realistic nightmare he just had. He recalls that the doorstep the boy stood on looked all too familiar.

He clears his throat and Sir Henry turns to him. He chuckles. "My goodness, I had no idea what time it was. How did you sneak past me anyway?"

Barloc walks over, sitting in the armchair near the fireplace. "I had another dream."

Sir Henry continues writing, focused on the task at hand. "It has been a moment since you have had these visions. What was this one about?"

Barloc takes in a shaky breath. "I found a bone in the field while farming. Had something to do with that. What was this place, before you owned it?"

No reaction from the man, as he folds a flyer into an envelope. "When you don't have a lot of money, you don't ask questions about what property you can afford. The bone you found could have been from one of my animals that didn't escape the fire years ago. Could be anything."

Barloc lets out a snort of derision. "I mean, you have to admit, the fact that you are here before me is something outside of the natural order. You never were concerned about the history of this land? What could have happened here? The slightest bit superstitious about what stays behind?"

Sir Henry puts down his pen and turns to his companion. He is silent before choosing his words. "We are all haunted by something. Perhaps there are reasons, more so than what I was doing here, about why people did not like my little corner of the world. I do not know. That is why I tried to do something good with it. Turn it into a home for the lost. You cannot let the past dictate where you are going when moving forward."

With this statement, Sir Henry turns and continues with his clerical task. Barloc does not feel any better about it, but he realizes that this conversation will not proceed with any information he can utilize further to put his mind at ease.

He wishes the host of the house a good evening and retires to his room. He does not return directly to his bed, however.

Barloc looks out over the field he spent a better half of two days tilling. The moon is particularly bright this evening, and it luminates the grounds of Sir Henry's property.

He takes some time to mentally rationalize. Maybe the dream was subconscious guilt manifesting into a nightmare. He was spending so much time on this project and his mind was trying to scare him off to retreat back to more normal things to do. After all, none of what was happening in this new life was normal.

Nevertheless, he knew Sir Henry still needed his help, and that he needed rest. Before turning to his bed, he catches sight of something out the window moving in the grass. Draped in moonlight, a black cat wanders the grounds.

The cat turns and meets the gaze of Barloc. The creature regards the man with its silver eyes before it scurries into the nearby woods.

Barloc knew in his right mind that something about this land was off. His heart, however, knew that he must endure.

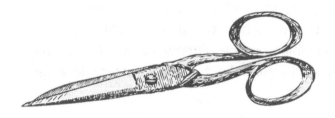

CHAPTER 2
Poppy

October 27th, 1929

Little Penelope Harris plays with her marionette puppets on the front lawn of the Schwartz Funeral Home.

While some may regard the scene as rather morbid, the townsfolk find this a common sight. Penelope lives here with her father Charles, the proprietor. Schwartz was the name of his business partner who succumbed to the Spanish Flu years earlier. He kept the name as a tribute to his old friend.

Penelope wears a jacket to keep the chilly air away. It is quiet now, but there was a flurry of activity days prior. There have not been many visitors recently, but a man in a top hat and a large woman wearing a shawl wrapped all around her came in for services.

She remembers her father, who always taught the little girl to be open about the concept of death, showing her the body of a pretty young woman, covered except for the neck up. He used it as a teaching lesson to not go out by herself. She remembers him looking over the police report, scoffing, and muttering "heart attack, my left foot."

This was a rare instance where Penelope remembers her father in control. This year has not been kind to their family, and he has begun to slowly unravel. The story goes, and the reason why people would not use his services any longer, was that he buried his family alive and had gone crazy. She remembers how he flew off in a rage when he saw the newspaper headline "SHUTDOWN LOOMS OVER FUNERAL HOME."

The truth of the matter was that her brother was sick from diptheria, and that her mother soon contracted it as well, since she was caring for him in close quarters. While there was a vaccine available, Boggy Meadow was so remote and they had so little money that regular healthcare was simply not a possibility. They had just enough to pay the mortgage on the funeral home property and for food.

Especially when the Great Depression started, business dried up. No one could afford funeral services - Charles heard that people were burning the bodies of deceased family members, or just leaving them wrapped in shrouds deep in the woods. Most could barely afford to run an obituary in the local paper.

Her brother and mother sadly perished in the home, and in the days before their death, she recalls him always covering his mouth with an old wash rag tied around his head. He constructed a tent for her outside and when she asked why she could not come in, he said something about miasma in the air and it was not safe. It was all a blur for the 12 year old girl. Such tragedy at a young age.

Despite the horrible rumors, she knew her father did not bury anyone alive. He brought their bodies outside, placed a bedsheet on the picnic table, and washed them in the fresh. He did not want to embalm them and aspirate any bacteria into the air. She helped dress them both and he loaded them into the modest caskets. She recalls helping to dig the family plot. The splinters in her hands and dirt under her fingernails from the old shovels.

The months that followed were filled with a silence she remembered quite well. She would help with chores to keep the place tidy, as her father took solace in liquor and ignored his responsibilities. Trash bins filled with empty bottles, rotten food and unopened mail.

On this day, however, everything changed. She was hopeful that the pretty woman's recent funeral would turn things around. They had some money and soon, other ceremonies would follow.

After collecting her puppets, she walks inside to the kitchen and notices her father sitting at the table. His back is to her, breathing heavily through his nose. He holds a bottle tightly in his right hand and angrily slams down a small batch of papers with the left. He tosses the bottle to the ground and it shatters. She covers her mouth, so as not to make noise.

She remains silent as she watches him forcefully stand, the chair toppling backwards to the floor with a loud bang. He walks off in a hurry, and when the coast is clear, she tiptoes to the table to see what he was reading that made him so mad. She picks two sheets of paper up - one is a sheet from the bank that says FORECLOSURE, and the other is a letter from something called The Children's Bureau. She is not certain what either means, but it could not be good.

She retreats to her room and spends time either reading, making crafts or playing with her puppets. As night falls, she is hungry but she does not want to go back down into the kitchen. The violent, foreign behavior she saw earlier gave her a fright. Best to stay put.

When she becomes too tired to stay awake any longer, she puts her puppets away on the nightstand and starts to work on picking up her crafting supplies. When she turns, she is startled by the doorknob turning.

As the door creaks open, she sees her father, disheveled and holding another bottle. He can barely stand straight. "Poppy," he mutters drunkenly.

This had always been her nickname, but ever since all of the hardships their family had endured this year, she had not heard him say it in a long time. There was nothing joyful about this greeting, though. "Yes, father?"

He stumbles towards her and she backs up slightly. "They're gonna take you away from me. They're taking the home, too," he says, tears in his eyes.

His disgusting breath wafts into Penelope's nose. It is similar to the chemicals he uses in embalming, but not as clean. She backs up further. "Who? Who is?"

He closes the gap between them and puts both hands on her cheeks, stroking them with his thumbs. He chokes back a sob. "It's better this way," he says.

She does not have time to think about what this means, as he swiftly moves his hands from her face to her neck. He wrenches his hands and applies pressure. She struggles to breathe, pounding her fists at his arms. She tries to kick him, but her small stature combined with his unsteady gait causes them both to tumble on the floor.

She is free of his clumsy grip for a moment and gasps for air, coughing. He looks up at her and crawls forward, a blank expression on his face. "All my family is dead. Let it all die then," he grumbles, in a drunken stupor.

She looks around, tears blurring her vision. Her heart is pounding in her ears. When he gets close and is able to get one hand around her throat, she blindly reaches behind her. She brushes her fingers against the cold metal of the handles, grabs, and shoves a closed pair of crafting scissors into the back of his neck.

He wails in pain and sits upright to pull them out, blood coating his hands. She takes the opportunity to get away, running down the stairs, out the door, and into the woods behind the funeral home.

She walks for hours but it feels like days. She sobs until her stomach hurts. Her throat burns from crying and the physical altercation earlier. She finally sees light glowing in the distance and goes toward it. Moth to a flame.

She views an archway and a gate. She walks up to the gate and wraps her little hands around the bars. Inside, a woman sits on a blanket in front of a fire pit, a shawl wrapped around her. She meets the gaze of the little girl. The lady has a beard on her face, which would otherwise be an odd thing to see, but Penelope is too traumatized to care.

"You okay, honey?" The young girl shakes her head at the inquiry, and tries to speak, but her windpipe was damaged from the turmoil of the night. The bearded woman walks toward the gate, telling the little one to watch her fingers as she pulls it open. She regards the small child, noticing the marks on her neck, specks of blood on her outfit, and dried tears on her cheeks. She sighs.

"You ever had a s'more, little one?" Penelope shakes her head. "Well, you are in for a treat! I just heard of these and they are my new favorite midnight snack. It's chocolate and graham cracker, and you glue them together with a hot marshmallow." She leans forward and whispers. "I usually don't share them, but it looks like you had a bad day. Would you like one?" A nod is her answer.

By a warm fire in the dark, quiet night, the child and the woman sit, eating their treats. The lady looks upon her young guest. "You can stay here for a little while, if you want. If anyone asks, tell them Galinda said it was okay."

Penelope struggles to speak. "Thank you."

***

Late Spring, 1933.

Mr. Barloc looks up at an old, impending house. There is a "for sale" sign sticking in the ground outside the property, but it has long since laid dormant. He walks up the path and sees a door, boarded up with a bank notice tacked upon it. The sound of crickets from the woods echoes in the early evening.

He knows he won't be able to enter here and further surveys his surroundings. Though the home is abandoned and the bushes around the perimeter are overgrown, there is one window where there are no shrubs underneath. In fact, this patch of ground looks rather fresh. He looks closer and sees footprints. He puts his hands on the window's glass and pushes upward, opening the window with a vicious creaking noise.

He carefully climbs into the old house. He notices that though there are certainly cobwebs and the home is pitch dark within, it was mostly kept up with. He sees there are wooden boards nailed to the entrance of the stairway, and that the effort to climb over them to get upstairs would be too much. He takes his lantern he carried in through the window and explores further.

In what would be the dining room, there is a dresser, candles, and a bed. A bedsheet is nailed to the wall over the window in this room. There are two stacks of books on the floor, and the dresser has marionette puppets hanging from hooks.

He continues forward, passing by a door in the hall that is also boarded up with a sign that says EMBALMING on it. He eventually comes upon the kitchen. On the table, he finds a bowl with an apple and an orange in it, horribly bruised but still looking edible. On the table, there are more candles, a pair of rusted, stained scissors, and a newspaper clipping dated November 5th, 1929. He moves the lantern over it to read the text.

"UNDERTAKER FOUND DEAD, CHILD FEARED KIDNAPPED"

He hears footsteps behind him and turns. A young girl in her early teens looks back at him. She is dirty and malnourished. She wears what looks like an older woman's clothes that are too big for her. She holds a basket of moldy food.

She is startled by this stranger in her home and steps back a bit. "Don't be afraid," he says softly, putting the lantern down on the table. "I like your shoes. They're nice for a young lady."

She looks down at her lace-up Cuban heels, caked in dried mud, then back up at his glance. "They belonged to my mother," she says quietly.

He pulls out a chair and sits, continuing to face her. "I know it may sound odd, but I had a dream, and it led me here." He looks around, then back at her. "Have you been living here alone for a long time?"

She puts down the basket of food, wrings her hands anxiously, and nods. "You're not in trouble dear. Not at all. In fact, I wanted to offer to bring you somewhere safe."

The girl looks up at him, her eyes glittering with tears. "Are you the Boogeyman?" Mr. Barloc furrows his brow. "Who?"

She looks around nervously before answering. "Whenever I am in the woods to fetch water, or in town gathering food, I see him following me. He wears a dark coat. He almost got me once, but I ran away."

Because she is young and has been alone for a prolonged period of time, he figures she was suffering from paranoia, or an overactive imagination. "No my dear, I am not here to hurt you. I'm here to help. Tell me, have you heard of Sir Henry's?"

She nods. "The old place in the hills. I went there once before. I tried to go back again, but everyone was gone and the gate was locked up. I heard it burned down, so I wanted to see for myself."

He looks upon her basket of old food. "Just how do you find things to eat?" She turns away from his eye contact, ashamed. "They throw out a lot of food behind the market in town. Can't let it go to waste."

He sighs. "Well, you don't have to do that anymore. As long as you pitch in, which it certainly looks like you keep things clean with limited resources, you earn your keep. You'll have a warm place to sleep, you can get a bath, and good food."

She looks up and a small smile appears. "S'mores?" He smiles back at her. "That can be arranged."

He reaches out a hand. "I'm Mr. Barloc. What's your name?" She hesitantly reaches out, and meets him with a feeble handshake. "I'm Poppy."

CHAPTER 3
Vex

Early Summer, 1933.

A teenage girl walks home from school in the rain. As always, she keeps her head down to avoid eye contact with others. She usually takes the long way home through the woods, but the rain is heavy and she can barely see the path in front of her.

She is not in a hurry to get home as she walks along the road. Her father escaped to the big city after the divorce, no siblings to turn to, and her mother was not a kind-hearted person. She grips her wooden umbrella handle tight as hail soon starts joining the falling rain.

She was hardly spoken to at home, was rarely called upon by teachers, and was always given hurtful nicknames by the other children. Sometimes, she could not even remember her own name until she would write it down for homework assignments. This unfortunate girl suffered from Cushing Syndrome, and other than fluctuating weight issues, her teeth have always been crooked. She shudders at a loud clap of thunder, her shoes soaking.

"Hey piggy, eat dirt!" She turns toward the insult that was hurled her way. A group of boys, unbothered by the weather, peddle their bicycles towards her. Her breath picks up into a pant as she struggles to hold both her parasol and school supplies. As they come closer, she loses grip of the books. She lets out a moan of sadness as they land in the mud, but she keeps jogging.

They are now directly cycling next to her on the left side, and she starts to veer off into the woods to her right to escape them. "Oink oink!" One of the boys lets out the cruel taunt as he tosses a rock at her.

As the rock collides with her shoulder, she screams as she takes a tumble down a short hill. When she lands, she is covered in a mixture of leaves and dirt. She checks herself for any major injuries and other than scratches, looks to be okay. She regards her umbrella, the canopy and ribs of the top bent and twisted from the fall. "Oh, great-"

Her statement of aggravation is interrupted by a bolt of lightning striking her umbrella. The jolt of electricity causes a blinding flash all around her and a deafening boom.

The heat moves about her body in a sickening fashion. She convulses from the force of it. The ground vibrates beneath her torso, thrumming up her legs, chest, and arms. Her right arm holding the umbrella shakes with a mighty force, a constant burning pulse.

Her heart works overtime to pump blood, but she passes out from the shock of the strike. As she falls to the soil, hail and rain cover her unconscious body.

***

The young girl awakens in the night. She blinks slowly and tries to register where she is. The moon peeks out from the trees. Humidity in the air, wet grass beneath her, and the smell of burnt flesh.

She slowly stirs, evaluating her physical state. She feels stiff, but there is no pain similar to burns. She is thirsty, so she sits fully up, and is able to stand - wobbly but still in control of her range in motion.

She walks cautiously until she hears the sound of running water nearby. Once she reaches the creek, she cups her hands to scoop up a drink of water, but regards her appearance first. She has black, burnt flesh from her eyes down to her cheeks.

The tips of her teeth have shattered at the edges from the impact of the lightning strike. Her hair, once a dirty blonde, is now a shiny black color. After accepting that she can deal with her injuries later, she takes multiple gulps of water.

She goes back to find her belongings, retracing her steps. She grabs her umbrella - the wooden handle still stable but any part of the canopy burnt away except for the metal ribs, now curled up almost into a claw-like shape.

She trudges back up the hill that she fell down earlier and revisits the road, seeking out her books. When she finds them, she tries to pluck them out of the mud, but it has since dried, now partially buried in the hard dirt.

She feels anger take over. *Why was everything so unfair?!* She growls and strikes the umbrella into the Earth, electricity bubbling from the metal spokes and shooting into the tree above.

She gasps and looks up - the branch overhead on fire from the impact of the energy ball. She regards her umbrella, now some sort of divining rod. This energy manifested due to embracing her heavy emotions, instead of her usual instinct of swallowing them down.

She walks forward, still dazed, and eventually comes upon buildings. Outside of the town hall, past the Irving Family memorial gazebo, she sees three bikes scattered carelessly to the ground. She hears the laughter of boys. Her anger grows. The crackling sound of buzzing hums from the end of her staff.

She continues her march and sees her harassers at the town's bulletin board. "What is this?" "Garbage!" One of the boys crumples a piece of paper and tosses it on the ground. It lands at her feet, and their shocked gazes meet hers. She saunters towards them. Two of them are still frightened, while the third lets out a mean chuckle. "Hey look, more garbage! Aren't you lost, freakshow?"

She smiles, tilting her head and letting her row of sharp, jagged teeth show. *They don't recognize me. Good.* She starts to point her staff towards them, an electric current swirling between the spokes of metal. She continues to let the power compile as two of the boys run away. She hurls the ball of energy towards the boy who earlier tossed the rock at her, which had changed the course of her life forever.

A loud blast rings in the night. Wood splinters and lands on the ground. When the smoke clears, the door of the town hall has a gaping chasm kissed with flames. The impact was just to the left side of the stunned boy's head. He sits while gasping in fear, unable to move, his chest heaving.

She charges toward him and holds him down with one hand. She holds the staff to his face. The sputtering light of electricity reflects in his terrified eyes and the sizzle of burnt wood fills his nostrils. He feels the sting of the static energy as it hovers just above his skin.

"You shall never vex anyone again, do you hear me?" He nods furiously, in return. "Yes, I'm sorry, I'm sorry."

She smiles, licks at her sharp teeth, and stares menacingly at him. "I'll let you leave with your pathetic little life, but if you ever hurt anyone again, I will turn you into a pile of ashes."

She hisses the final word like a snake and forcefully releases him, his head knocking into the wood behind him. The thrust of movement causes him to chomp down on his own lip, blood pouring down his shirt. He starts sobbing and runs away, grabbing one of the abandoned bikes and riding off into the night.

When it is once again quiet, she walks over to the discarded paper, unfurling and reading it.

Along with his menagerie of misfits, they seek their revenge on the judgmental living who have cast them out.

No one ever saw the mistreated teenage girl ever again. It was assumed she perished in the storm, but there were no resources for a search party and the family only wanted to foot the bill for an obituary.

Two things did happen, however. Sir Henry's gained another family member. The children of Boggy Meadow also knew that if you did anything wrong, whether it was picking on other children, neglecting your chores, or walking home by yourself, you would have to answer to a creature named Vex.

CHAPTER 4
Beatrice

Late Summer, 1933.

In the cool early morning, the sun merely peaking over the horizon, Mr. Barloc packs up his vehicle. Sir Henry hands him a leather suitcase, the last item that the trunk is loaded with. When it is safely closed and locked, the two men face each other.

"Hate to see you go, my friend," Sir Henry states. He reaches out for a hand shake, but after looking down at his bony hand, he quickly moves it back to his side.

Barloc forcefully exhales. "I do regret leaving, but I have affairs to take care of in the city."

Sir Henry regards his colleague, a serious look in his eyes. "It's more than that. I can see it."

Barloc turns his gaze to the road outside of the estate, biting his lip anxiously. "You look like you haven't slept in weeks, you've lost weight, and you're a nervous wreck. Am I that bad of a host?"

Barloc laughs slightly, then lets out a ragged sigh. He meets the eyes of Sir Henry, and shrugs. "The visions have been more real, and more frequent than ever, living out here. I know there is a purpose to it, but the more I give of myself, the more of myself I lose. I don't know how to explain it, but I feel if I distance myself, it will help. I hope."

There is silence between them, until Barloc scoffs. "Plus, there is not a decent bagel within miles of here! If that's not reason enough to get back to the city, what is?" They both share a brief chuckle, then Barloc holds out his palm. Sir Henry grips his colleague's hand, shriveled cold flesh meeting warm, healthy skin. "We made sure everything was taken care of. Until I can return once more, I will send letters and find some investors for the place." Sir Henry nods as the handshake ends. "God speed."

Sir Henry watches his companion load himself into the car, drive past the gates and onto the road. As he grabs the gate handle to close it, a small shadow zips between his legs. He turns and witnesses a black cat running up to his front steps, jumping up to a windowsill and squeezing itself inside of his home. He grunts in frustration, closing and locking the gate.

He makes his way back up to his house and once inside, he scans with his eyes. "Where did it go?" He hears a clatter in the kitchen, grabs a broom from the cleaning closet in the hall, and approaches. "You better not have fleas, you grimy little intruder."

"Awfully judgemental for someone who doesn't even have skin." Sir Henry gasps. He seeks out the voice and drops his broom in shock. A young woman sits at his kitchen table.

She is beautiful, draped in a black shroud with dark curly hair and staggering silver eyes. She lifts an eyebrow at him and places her hands on the table. A cockroach exits her left sleeve and crawls across the surface.

"Who are you? How did you get into my house?"

She chuckles. "I am many things, but I suppose you can call me Beatrice. Likely all your feeble mind can comprehend."

He slowly walks near her, noting there is what he could describe as a slight mist around her that slightly blurs her appearance. "You intrude in my home and insult me? Are you mad?"

She leans forward, placing one hand over the other with her elbows resting on the table. "I heard legends about the Phantom of the Great Sir Henry. I came here to prove it was some tourist scam. How surprised I am to be wrong."

He scoffs. "Okay, you can read an address on a flyer. Good for you, madam. What right does that give you-"

"Enough talk!" With her abrupt exclamation, she lifts a hand and a cloud of debris starts to drift from her sleeve. The dust circles around her, similar to the motion of a tornado, whipping violent wind around Sir Henry's kitchen. He grips the wall until the wind dissipates.

When the dust clears, retreating back into her sleeve, he is confused and frightened by her sudden change in appearance. Long, limp hair with a pointed nose and pale, wrinkled skin. She smirks, rotten teeth under her aged lips.

"I was trying to be cordial but that old charade is just so exhausting," she utters in a cocky manner.

"What do you want? Are you the Grim Reaper? Have you come for me?" Sir Henry states, a hint of fear in his voice.

She tilts her head back and cackles, then meets his gaze. "Sit, and I will tell you why I am here."

He cautiously approaches the kitchen table, pulls a chair back and seats himself, keeping a distance between them. Her ashen eyes regard him, leering all the while.

"Many years ago, in the seventeenth century, I was living in a small town in the northeast. It was near the ocean and within nature, all at once. It was the ideal place for myself, along with my Pagan brothers and sisters."

He feels internal panic. "You're a witch, then?" She snickers. "Quiet boy, it's rude to interrupt the elderly," she croaks, in response.

She takes in a deep breath and when she exhales, the scent of moss and grass seeps out of her mouth. "I should have just been satisfied with bettering myself, but like a fool, I fell for a mortal man. He was so charming, warm and open," sadness glitters in her eyes. "But then, news came from Salem about the danger of witches. The horrible things happening there."

She furrows her brow in anger, breaking eye contact. "I was in the woods with my brethren, performing a spell of protection, but he followed me. He saw what we were doing and he told the local villagers." Fire slowly starts to billow from her fingertips as her fury grows. "He was supposed to be different, and in the end, he put us all at the end of a noose."

Sir Henry struggled to find the words to say. "I am sorry that happened, but I fail to understand what this has to do with me."

She scoffs and shakes her head. "Typical mortal, so impatient."

He slams a fist down on the table. "Look at me - do I look 'mortal' to you? Did you have something to do with what I've become? Talk, witch."

She stares at him, a snake slithering from under her sleeve. The serpent hisses at him, teeth dripping with venom. "Yes, he called me that, too. Your paternal ancestor. Yet another ignorant patriarch. The one who sent us to the gallows. Little did they know that I was able to finish my protection spell. They made the error of saving my hanging for last. Stuck in that dank cell, I taught myself to transmogrify, and escaped right out from under them. My spell allows me to only live long enough to see your bloodline snuffed out for your transgressions."

The snake lunges forward and bites Sir Henry's arm. He just regards the creature, having no reaction, and lifts his head. "Sorry to disappoint, and thank you for the charming exposition, but I don't think that will work," he says, annoyed at the attack.

The snake unlatches and retreats back from whence it came. "I know, I was just hoping it would hurt. No luck, I see." She taps her fingers impatiently on the table.

"Every misfortune that happened to your family was because of me. Your bloodline was rotten, so I simply helped speed up the decay. Despite all the miscarriages, accidents and illnesses, you all sadly continued to flourish until the late nineteenth century when it was just down to one cluster of you," she snarls, holding up one decrepit finger. "One man, one woman, and two children."

Sir Henry shakes his head. "I think you have me mistaken for someone else then, as I am an only child."

She pouts her lower lip in a condescending fashion. "Aw, someone's parents did not tell the whole truth, did they?" She puts a hand up her sleeve and pulls out an old photo, sliding it across the table. She points to a baby in a woman's arms. "That is you, and your original family. Before you were displaced."

He looks upon the photo, trying to comprehend the news. It couldn't be. Two adults he does not recognize. There is a young boy who is also pictured, no older than a toddler, as he is able to stand on his own. He has a slight scar on his cheek. Everyone in the photo wears clothing of the working class.

"Had you not wondered why you could never find your birth certificate," she snarls. "Or why your hair color was different from your parents when you were growing up?"

He looks up at her, the rage building. "So you're responsible for killing my Bride then?"

She shrugs. "Not directly. I cannot take credit for all of your afflictions. For some reason, you have been able to sidestep my curse quite a bit, like a clever rat avoiding a trap," she states with indignation in her voice.

"Finding a caring family not of your bloodline was the first sickening event I had to suffer through. All of your business success, and then your happy little marriage. You can imagine how infuriating that was for me to sit by and watch."

He glares at her. "Did you set fire to my barn and kill my Bride all those years ago? I will not. Ask. Again," he says, magnifying each word with a slight pause in between.

"You still think you're calling the shots here?" He looks down as a group of ants carries the photo back into her hand, retreating up her sleeve. She grips the photograph, crumpling the aged paper. The fire of her fingertips spreads amongst her balled-up fist, setting the item ablaze.

"Turns out, you are not the last of your lineage, as I had hoped. I was desperate and sought divination. Eventually, I discovered that your purpose is to take your brother's life. You specifically," she states, unfurling her hand and letting the ashes of the photo float to the ground. "Once you do, you will be able to pass on to the afterlife, and my spell will finally be complete. I can at last become one with the Earth."

"Why me?" Sir Henry states, continuing to try and digest all of the information he was given in a short period of time.

"I do not make the rules. Blood for blood," she answers, plainly. "This is your only purpose for returning from the grave. How does the Bible go - 'an eye for an eye, and a tooth for a tooth,' as they say? Then again, I've never had much interest in the scripture of man. To put it in simplest terms, since I am tired of repeating myself, your end equals my end, and I would quite like to finally be at rest. Understand?"

He shakes his head. "I can't do it. I cannot take another man's life. Especially one I never met. Not just based on some tall tale."

She cocks an eyebrow. "Not even for a murderer? He took men, women, even children. Why am I not surprised someone from your family would commit such putrid acts?"

He huffs in anger. "I've had quite enough of your parlor tricks and cruel words. Especially your blasphemy earlier. Not in my home."

She lets out another evil cackle. "You still believe in God, after everything you've been through?"

His eyes begin to glint with tears. "There has to be some purpose to all this, and I refuse to believe it is to be an instrument of murder. I am not a monster, and I will not be manipulated by you, witch."

The sound of thunder suddenly echoes outside and rain violently pours down. Wind gusts forward, shattering Sir Henry's windows. A blast of broken glass, dead leaves and dirt enters his home. Beatrice surrounds herself with the debris, a cyclone of energy forming around her. She floats above the floor, her hair flowing around her head. Her gray eyes glow with fury and Sir Henry grips onto the table tightly to hang on.

"If you refuse to fulfill this destiny, the curse upon your family will continue, no matter how little of you remain," she bellows, her voice distorted and echoing. "If I cannot die, then you will suffer as long as I must remain alive to witness your end. Heed my words, Sir Henry - no one escapes their fate!"

Once her evil monologue reaches its end, the circle of rubble increases in speed and volume, concealing her. The force of the wind knocks Sir Henry backwards in his chair. He grunts and lets himself up once the supernatural squall dies down.

He pulls himself back up, making eye contact with the same black cat from earlier. Gray eyes leer at him and it hisses, jumping off of the table and dashing past him. He tries to grab the animal, but it is too fast. It darts out the window and vanishes into the woods.

Sir Henry looks around, feeling overwhelmed with both the physical and emotional litter he was left behind with. Nevertheless, it was always in his nature to endure.

Adversity was no stranger, and now that he had people on property to take care of once more, he knew his purpose was for more than malicious reasons. It had to be.

He sees the broom he dropped earlier before this mystic altercation took place. He bends down to pick it up, and quietly starts sweeping the mess. He just hoped that he could get it all cleaned up before anyone else wakes for the morning. He anticipates a busy day ahead.

CHAPTER 5
Kane

Early Autumn, 1933.

Sweets for my sweet, because you deserve the world, little rabbit.

Nathaniel Kane wakes from his dream. A flashback to gentler times. A moving picture that replays in his mind from time to time of his beloved sister placing her homemade candies in his wicker basket. His nose would twitch in an adorable fashion that reminded her of the rabbits in the fields beyond their home.

He allows himself to remember, if just for a moment, when the boy's youthful exuberance was restored in the light of a warm home, alongside sisterly adoration and a flicker of optimism. However, his current reality is this drab, cold orphanage. The truth is, his world had disappeared one night in a blaze of fire. An inferno ignited from the very oven that his sister had crafted the candies he so loved.

He remembers the taste of these treats, wrapped in bright red cellophane, and a nostalgic burst of childhood happiness briefly swells in his troubled mind. He then feels guilt, recalling the image of his burnt down home and the scarlet bloody sheets that covered the smoldering bodies. Red is now a conflicting color for the boy.

All that remains of the Kane family after that awful night is a small, quiet child, soot stricken and scarred by the inferno, both physically and mentally. They had wrapped the boy's face in a damp cloth, but even then it was known that the child would never be the same, his cherubic visage forever tainted.

He closes his eyes and remembers the emergency service workers struggling to load him into the fire carriage. They noticed Nathaniel clasping a wicker basket, filled with candies. They attempted to remove the items from the burned boy's grasp, but he struggled against them with a strength that was not possible from such a young, injured lad.

Even as he recovered, met with The Children's Bureau, and was transferred to the Castlemore orphanage, Nathaniel Kane kept a constant, determined grasp on the candy basket. It was his last bastion of a life before the flames. Rare recollections, ripe for consumption. After his foray into memories, Nathaniel forces himself out of bed and goes about his day.

Later in the afternoon, the unspoken trinity of Castlemore's wrath stalks the halls of this home for wayward young souls. Abel, Ned and Jude are a trio who have earned themselves a reputation around the orphanage for picking on the younger, smaller children. Bullies often crave attention - nectar for their troubled souls that slakes the flames of anger. The new arrival, the quiet boy with the covered face, was the new focus of their ire.

The brutes walk toward young Nathaniel, black textile wrapped around his head, allowing just the slightest partition for eye holes. The top of the fabric was fashioned into two points that stuck upwards like the ears of a rabbit. They watch him from the hall in the dining room as they plan their ambush. Lunch consists of roasted chicken and farm fresh vegetables, but the boy refuses his meal. He slides his tray to a little girl sitting near him and simply eats one single candy from his basket.

Abel is the largest, de facto leader, as the tyrant hierarchy tends to decree. As Nathaniel exits the dining room, he blocks the small boy's path. "What do we have here?" Abel's voice is deep for his age, an attribute he uses to maximize the effect of intimidating others.

"Hey, I'm talkin' to you," he sneers, as he receives no response. The brute reaches out and grasps the hood by one of the elongated ears, pulling the boy's face upward in order to make eye contact. "Now, that's better. What's your name, kid?"

The boy still does not answer. "I don't think the little gimp can talk," Ned states with a mean snort of laughter. "Let's pick out a name for him. Bunny Boy sounds good," Jude offers.

Abel smirks. "Well then, Bunny Boy, here's the thing: you're new here and you're looking to make friends I bet. Well, we'll be your friends, right fellas?" The other two murmur insincere grunts of agreement.

Abel rests a meaty paw on the young boy's slender shoulder. "What do you say, Bunny? You wanna be my friend?" Further silence. "I'm sorry, but I gotta say, you're not being very friendly to your new pals," Abel shakes his head in mock displeasure. "See, there are three things friends do: they talk to each other, they show their faces, and they share."

He tugs right on the hood's ears and pulls the dark material up, tearing the fabric in the process. The boy beneath the hood emits his first vocalization to the trio via a startled grunt. His small hands rise up to pull the hood back down, which causes him to drop his wicker basket in the process. The pile of red treats scatter about haphazardly.

"Alright, free candy!" Ned bellows. "Thanks, chump!" The three thugs drop to the floor and grab at the small red baubles, stuffing them into their pockets. Abel glances up at the boy and recoils at his exposed lower jaw. The child's face, once concealed, is a patchwork of scar tissue and melted flesh. "Oh gross! No wonder you wear that stupid thing! Let's go guys, before Bunny Boy gets us sick with whatever he has."

The three ruffians depart with pockets full of sweets and hearts full of hatred, leaving behind the broken husk of their handiwork. Nathaniel sobs to himself as he pulls the ruined hood back over his face. He drops to the ground and scrounges about frantically, desperate gasps emitting from smoke-tarnished lungs. A wrinkled, gentle hand suddenly meets his own. It grasps his own hand softly and presses a single candy into his clutch.

Nathaniel looks up, expecting to see his sister smiling at him from Heaven. No such luck, but this angel was older and very much Earthbound. The head mistress of the orphanage pulls the boy close, his basket still on the floor, and she cradles the sobbing boy in a hug.

***

The next day, Nathaniel sits on the edge of his bed. His nose twitches as he plucks at the stitches with a slender finger, feeling the frayed cloth beneath his touch. The old woman had performed admirably, repairing his hood and mending both the fabric and the boy's spirit the day prior.

He holds onto his last candy, the single remaining vestige from his previous life. It was precious, unique and he wished for more. He craved what he had lost, yet he also acknowledged that there was no way to find it, lost forever to time and tarnish.

Footsteps resound on old floorboards and Nathaniel pulls his hood back over his scarred face. The three larger tormentors from before approach, and the small boy stiffens beneath his hood, shards of fear creeping along his flesh. Abel kneels before the Kane child, the floor creaking beneath his bulk. "Happy Halloween, buddy." He holds out a plump hand upon which rests a single, red wrapped sweet.

Was it really Halloween already? The very concept of time had been lost to the young lad, yet he suddenly finds himself faced with the revelation of All Hallow's Eve and the suspicious generosity of his newly christened rival. Abel reaches out and places the candy in the wicker hamper.

"Listen, the boys and I, well, we came up here to apologize. Ain't that right?" Ned and Jude nod and grumble under their breath. "We were mean to you for no reason. So we wanna make it up to you."

Nathaniel stares back, doubt reigning over reason. "What if I told you that I could get you more candy? Better than trick-or-treating. We could all get piles of sweets, just like those ones that you have in your little basket there."

The hooded child tilts his head with intrigue. "We wanna show you the Candy Tree. Never heard of it, have you? I'm not surprised, it's a bit of a secret. So keep this between us guys, us good buddies. The Candy Tree is really special. One night a year, we figured out how to make candy rain from the sky."

Nathaniel glances down at his barren basket. He wants to hold onto his memories, his family. He knows he might be striding into dangerous territory, but his want and desire eclipses all notion of rationale. The desires of his young, scarred heart were just too strong.

***

"There it is: the Candy Tree." After some time walking in the cold dark night, there it stood before them. Ned gestures his lantern towards the old fork in the road before them. The quartet had quickly escaped Castlemore just as the old woman had begun her rounds, checking to make sure all the children were accounted for.

The old oak is stately, illuminated in the light of a quarter moon peeking shyly from between tumultuous clouds overhead. The lantern light casts a pall of amber upon the black tree-flesh.

The stout boy guides the smaller child closer to the tree as his other two cohorts tag along. At the apex of the crossroads, all signs of civilization are swallowed whole by the inky maw of the unknown. A gust of wind blows through the night and the old tree creaks under the strain of the tempest.

Nathaniel approaches the ancient tree. Carved into the side of the mighty trunk is a massive furrow, a good sized portion of bark stripped away by some powerful impact. *Lightning? An accident?* Misfortune, not unlike that which had baptized the poor boy in fire, birthing him into a new life.

The tree reminded him of the holidays, much like this evening of Halloween. Days plucked from the calendar for ancient celebrations - death and renewal, indulgence and family. All coalescing into something unique, grand and imposing. All the days branching together, roots to nourish the very soul of humanity. Roots connecting to the tree that held the key to all that he had wanted.

"The tree has scars just like you do. It waits for kids like us that have lost stuff in the world, as a trade off for the candy. The boys and I have already taken our turns, so without you, there would be no candy. All you gotta do is give the tree a hug. When you do that, we will be up to our necks in sweets," Abel explains.

Nathaniel clutches his basket tight to his small frame. He had only ever set it aside to bathe. Even the dream world couldn't tear it from his grasp, as he slept with it under his covers. Yet, for the second time in two days, he releases his grip - this time, on his own volition rather than it being snatched cruelly away.

The boy's slender arms wrap around a small portion of the colossal trunk. The oak feels warm beneath his hands, pulsating every so slightly. Almost like a beating heart. It feels like life, and he runs his hands over the scars in the wood. He feels the tree hug him back, the grasp of its roots thin and rough, ragged to the touch. He closes his eyes and waits for the pitter-patter of goodies to rain from the sky.

After waiting a moment, he opens his eyes and pulls away from the tree to inspect the lack of candy. He suddenly finds he is stuck. He wrenches his face back and, through the eye holes in his mask, sees it was not the roots of the tree embracing him, but a cord of rope wrapping taut around himself and the mighty conifer. Nathaniel grunts and squeals with renewed vigor. He cannot escape, as his arms hold fast in an eternal embrace.

He feels a soft impact against his head, as the wicker basket is tossed at him and tumbles to the ground. His last two candies are gone. From his peripheral view, Nathaniel catches the slightest blush of an amber lantern light fading away. A cruel voice calls out, "Trick or treat, Bunny Boy! It ain't even Halloween yet - what a twit."

The voices of the trio begin to fade, as does their lantern light. All that is left is silence and darkness, not even the ethereal magic of All Hallow's to keep him warm. Just one small child tied to an old oak tree at the crossroads of the dead and the living. Nathaniel cries only for a moment as he feels the frost of the autumn chill seeping in. He closes his eyes and further leans his head against the trunk.

It no longer matters to him if it was the elements, wild animals, or the monsters rumored to wander these mysterious woods. He just hopes the night consumes him so he can once again be with his family and away from this vicious world.

***

The small boy wakes, his arms aching and body freezing. He feels the cord being loosened around him. He slumps against the Candy Tree before dropping to his rear alongside the trunk, sore all over.

His vision is blurry from exhaustion and the dark, but he looks up at his rescuer. He didn't know this girl. She slings the offending cord to the ground and gazes down at the boy, dark hair blowing lightly in the autumn breeze.

"I found you," she says. Her voice is a tinkling of frost against a bed of fallen autumn foliage. "I heard you crying." The boy shrinks back against the trunk, fearful of the stranger who approached him, but then the young woman presses the wicker basket into his hand. It was filled with his cherished red-wrapped candies. His eyes widened. How was it possible?

The girl pulls out a small pair of scissors, stained with an old, brown substance that gives the boy just the slightest of chills. She shakes off a frayed edge of the rope she had cut earlier and uses the blades to carve a slit into the wrapping of two pieces of candy. She eats one and holds the other out for the boy. He devours it hungrily and silently revels in the sweet familiarity.

The girl chews the candy, studying the boy. "You came from Castlemore, didn't you?" He looks up at her in shock. "I was there for a while. The folks at the freak show found out who I was from the local paper and turned me over to the police. I forgive them, but I just - I couldn't take it. Ran away and no one was able to find me. I was good at disappearing."

She consumes another candy, and smiles at him. "You don't need to go back there, if you don't wanna," the girl says. "I know the old lady who runs the place is nice, but I know somewhere else where you'll be welcome. You won't have to hide, or be ashamed. Being alone is awful - take it from someone who made it into an art form for years."

The boy licks his scarred lips from behind his mask and his nose twitches with excitement. He is understandably apprehensive after this recent betrayal. Yet there was something darkly alluring and majestic about her invitation. She has a kind energy like his sister, but she too was marred by trauma and understood his pain. The girl extends her hand to him, and he makes his decision.

He removes his mask, yet she does not flinch or recoil, her smiling expression unwavering. He folds the mask neatly atop his pile of candy. The quiet boy takes the girl's hand and the pair begins their walk down the dark road ahead.

The next morning, the bullies, ushered there by the town police and the lady caretaker of Castlemore, only found a cut rope alongside empty candy wrappers on the ground, and forever would wonder what happened to the disfigured boy who never spoke. Nary aware that he found a new life with his misfit family mere miles from the dreary orphanage.

"My name is Poppy. Sir Henry will want to meet you," the girl states, her breath hanging in the chilly night air. "What should I call you, when I introduce you to him?"

"Kane," says the scarred boy, grinning a red-stained smile.

CHAPTER 6
Pyrum

October, 1692

Some places are simply born bad. Parcels of land that reveal the worst in human nature, coated in topsoil of hatred and fear, nourished with the blood of the innocent and the damned. It turns the ground sour - a locale where even the most infernal entities fear to tread and gives rise to the darkest of stories. Tales whispered by frightened school children and superstitious adults.

These are the stomping grounds of legend incarnate, where every spoken word is a seed fit to germinate in the depths of depravity and the mire of sin. Each seed, ready to sprout and evoke countless terrors on any who would dare set foot within its reach. God have mercy, should you decide to settle there.

Boggy Meadow was such a place. A tiny patch of land on the edge of American civilization that played host to a compact collection of settlers. They staked their claims in a small village of rough hewn log cabins and rustic patchworks of a functioning society. To the East was Bill Tassel's farm and general store, the Church of the Holy Grounds to the South, more meadow land to the North, and the West was a place the people of this town didn't like to speak of often.

The Western Woods, a home of ash and elm trees spread thick and wide beyond the confines of the village, was formerly occupied by one Balthazar Bones. A man shunned by society, cast out by his own family to wander the wilderness and live a hermit's life. His sin was merely being born different.

By an unlucky roll of the genetic dice, Bones suffered from a positional skull deformity. His head developed into something vaguely pear shaped, more befitting a fruit or a vegetable than a man. Some of the locals took to referring to the man in the old tongue, dubbing the outcast as "Pyrum."

In as cruel a manner as judging his disability, he was declared the number one suspect in a series of slayings that occurred within the confines of the forest one cold October. Townsfolk were turning up massacred, torn limb from limb, so who better to persecute than the odd one out?

Balthazar Bones was swiftly captured on All Hallow's Eve and given his day in court. A trial which consisted solely of frightened townsfolk screaming curses and misdeeds in the hermit's direction. He was given no avenue for which to plead his case and, using the very trees and foliage of the Western Woods themselves, a pyre was swiftly built for which to execute the accused. Bill Tassel was given the grand honor of using a long staff carved from an elm log, lit aflame to ignite the execution fire. Mrs. Sarah Irving had volunteered to provide the flame, born from a candle lit within her traditional Jack-o-lantern.

Bones died that day in the flames of anger from a hate-plagued collective. As he choked on the ash, he cursed the ground upon which he burned. His words rang out in the night and rose into the sky, carried by clouds of smoke.

"You all had best embrace these flames! They will not hold my soul at rest for very long! I did nothing and yet, I burn, as wilt thou all," the man howled, his speech halted by a groan of pain. "Pyrum will return, oh yes. This I speak. When the flames are snuffed before the stroke of midnight, so too wilt thine pitiful lives. Mark my words, cowards!"

Bill Tassel thrust his pitchfork into the burning man to quiet his singed tongue. A rush of blood poured forth from the dying man, some of it eclipsing into the flames and the rest spattering into the soil before him. Sarah, blood speckling her dress, leaped back with a shriek, her pumpkin falling and smashing into shards upon the same ground. Orange seeds bathing in the ichor. Her husband Jeremiah ran to her aid and spat upon Balthazar Bones as he at last succumbed to the hateful inferno.

The townsfolk of Boggy Meadow left the morbid scene behind. A charred corpse to fall prey to the forest cravers of carrion. At last, the killer of the Western Woods would haunt them no longer. Or so they thought, as one week later, a local trapper caught and killed a particularly voracious black bear. Upon preparing the carcass for taxidermy, he discovered the remnants of the Ripper's alleged victims within its stomach.

Though fatally wrong, the townsfolk never spoke of this occurrence, nor did they return to the spot where they had burned an innocent man alive. Life quietly returned to normal in the village. Jeremiah and Sarah Irving found themselves expecting a child, Farmer Bill Tassel's pumpkin fields flourished and the sad, bloody saga of Balthazar Bones, the man with the pear shaped head, faded away into the mists of legend and the ages of obscurity.

***

October, 1702

Legend has a funny way of returning when it is not wanted. Children especially seem privy to the wonders of the world that lie beyond the rational, evoking the magic and allure of the unknown. Jacob Irving was particularly susceptible to this siren call. Old enough to learn the tales surrounding the woods from his classmates at the old wooden schoolhouse on the edge of town.

His mother Sarah would not be expecting him home for some time. She had only just begun to recover from the death of her husband, who had fallen ill and wasted away within their home. She had been spending more time with Farmer Bill, a fact which made the young lad cringe upon conjuring images of their dalliances together.

One foggy autumn day, he decided to venture beyond the threshold of the village. Towards the land forbidden amongst the elders and whispered about by his classmates.

Jacob nervously witnessed the Western Woods before him. He heard the stories. It would be nearly impossible for a boy in a small village to not have heard the tales.

"To bed before the shadows fall
make sure you stop and pray.
And if to the woods you should venture
bring fire to light your way.
Embrace the flames and keep them lit
God's gleam will grant you sight.
If before midnight, the fire dies

You'll succumb to Pyrum's blight.
He is mean and has no mercy
you better run and hide.
For when you're caught and he starts to carve
you'll wish you'd already died."

The boy shuddered upon recalling the rhyme, sung in mocking voices while children jumped rope. He was not a coward, though. He would prove it to no one but himself, as he took a deep breath and crossed into the forest ahead.

The woods are quiet, with the only sound being his footsteps upon freshly fallen leaves. The chill of autumn's ethereal embrace hangs in the crisp air, and he shudders in the cold. It does not take Jacob long to discover the remnants of the pyre, blackened and crumbling in a small clearing about a quarter mile beyond the tree line. Jacob takes a quick glance at the pile of blackened tree stumps and the greasy haze that seems to hover in the air. Ten years ago, the end of the Ripper of the Western Woods gave birth to a new legend.

He takes a step forward and his foot collides with something solid emerging from the fallen leaves. The boy bends low in the grey forest, fog curling about his shivering motions. He brushes away a small dusting of brown leaves and sees the charred human skull before him. It was oddly shaped, bent upright and elongated. The ground around it is crisp, stained black with a decade of forgotten sins.

A single brown spatter of dried liquid lay on the lower jaw of the skull. Most distressing is a curl of green, a spright of color emerging from the maw of blackened death. The tendril of a blooming plant spirals upwards from between the teeth, frozen in a scream of agony while sprouting new life into the world. As the boy kneels closer to observe in morbid curiosity, a single crimson drop of blood emerged from the tip of the plant. It drips softly on the dead leaves below and the black jaws of the skull close with a sudden clack.

Jacob falls back into the pile of refuse with a yelp and scurries out of the clearing. He dares not look back at the tableaux of black death and green life behind him, leaving the scene in a wisp of swirling fog that closed in and obscured it from his sight, but never from his memories.

He believed then, did the boy. As the sun slowly began to dip into the red autumn horizon, he felt another chill and remembered that a special day was swiftly approaching. Now more than ever, he must make time to carve a pumpkin so he can ward off the dead with the flames of grisly injustice.

When Jacob returns home, shivering from the cold, he finds relief in a crackling fire set by his mother. She sweeps him in and he notes that she smells of cider. She had likely been out with Farmer Bill, helping to plan his barn dance to be held the next night. It had been a bountiful year and Bill Tassel wanted to celebrate with the adults of the town.

Jacob sips at a bowl of soup and glances around their small dwelling. "Mother, where is the pumpkin? I require time to carve it before All Hallows Eve."

Sarah tilts her head and smiles at him from across the table. "There will be no pumpkin this year, my child."

Jacob drops his spoon into his soup in shock and gapes back at her, eyes wide with surprise. She senses his apprehension and sighs. "Farmer Bill decreed at the town hall that these schoolyard tales are a burden to our village. Pyrum this, Pyrum that. 'Tis nonsense. The pumpkins will be eaten, not used as props for childish stories, Jacob. Do not worry, my boy. Have faith that there is nothing to fear on All Hallows Eve."

He nods, retrieves the utensil he dropped, wipes it off with a cloth napkin, and resumes his meal. Yet in the back of his mind, he could not but feel that the old farmer on the edge of town was wrong.

***

Dreams came later that night to the troubled boy. Images danced about maniacally with fitful starts and wild pulses. Images of rotted remains overgrown with grasping foliage and drops of blood sprinkling from above.

Nourishment for crops, red life to the old dirt to give way to something ancient, angry. Something held at bay only by the light of the seasonal flames, but lurking just beyond its wicked grasp. Reaching forth with ragged claws to clutch the boy and drag him under.

When he woke, he knew what he had to do. He would not take any chances. Early in the morning, his mother had taken him to visit the farm and help pick vegetables for supper. Jacob snuck away and found baskets of plump orange gourds, hidden behind a shed, and grabbed the first one he could find. He took off with the hefty pumpkin, sneaking past the barn and making his way home.

The barn he dashed past was awash in colorful bunting and freshly dipped candles ready to cast warm, illuminating lighting on the evening's festivities. The Harvest Dance was to be held there later tonight, and the boy knew his mother would certainly be attending. It would be the perfect time for him to carve out the face on the pumpkin and make sure it was lit before the stroke of midnight. Then, all he had to do was keep the flame alive until October dispersed into the crisp autumn wind.

When his mother returned home that morning, she had grabbed the boy forcefully by the shoulders, admonishing him for running off without letting her know where he went. He was punished to stay in his room the rest of the day with no supper, and this was just fine for the young boy. Tonight, he would guard the leering face of the Jack-o-lantern to cast away those who might wish him harm.

***

Later that night, the festivities at Farmer Bill's barn are in full effect. All of the town's children are tucked in early so the adults can join the raucous din. Yet the cautious Jacob quickly escapes the covers of his bed, retrieving the gourd sequestered beneath his mattress. Due to her lingering anger at the boy's insolence, she never found the stolen pumpkin he grabbed earlier that day. She never even came up to say goodnight to him before leaving for the celebration.

Now, alone with only the stillness of the autumn night, Jacob set about carving. He uses a long, curved knife to remove the moist innards and creates a puddle of orange seed-laden detritus in the process. His end result is a rather jagged and haphazard, but effective, toothy maw of a Jack-o-lantern.

He swiftly lights a long, white wick candle and places it inside the hollowed out interior. The boy carries the glowing gourd out to the front walk of their small cottage. Here, he places the blazing guardian to his side and waits. It is the only light set to illuminate the otherwise abysmal, dark night in Boggy Meadow. The peace is disrupted by the echoing yells from the adults celebrating in the barn. Jacob could swear that the laughter sounded more like screams, but what could they have to shriek about other than a night of jubilation?

***

Further beyond the boundaries of Boggy Meadow, it became all too clear that legends hide a seed of truth deep within their pulpy confines. On this night of mirth, magic and frolic, something waited beneath the sour soil. There existed a bare patch in the Western Woods where plants dared not to grow, save for one stubborn yet ethereal sprout. The green began to intertwine with something black and rotted. Life unto death emerging beneath blood-tainted Earth.

The new life bursts forth, steeped in the fires of vengeance and the anguish of injustice. A seed germinating and sprouting into a misshapen orange gourd. A bulbous, leering grin tapered off to a pinched top, forming a distinctive shape that years prior had fallen to the flames. The new life growls, enshrouded in vines with reformed limbs composed of writhing green matter, tearing away from the ground. Glancing about at surroundings and turning toward a pile of burned timber, dirt crumbling off with every movement. The new life drops to creaking knees and runs grasping tendrils along the ashes, groaning in anger as memories flood back.

Thrashing arms come upon a long stick, charred and gummed. Raising the staff into the air, mental reminders of being set aflame and thrust into a formerly flesh-laden form. The burning, the sobbing, the cursing. Hatred reborn, sprouting forth to taint the night and lay waste to those who had sinned against an innocent soul.

Years have passed when children had lit lanterns to ward off the one who lurked in the woods, but this year, it senses only a single solitary flame. Not enough old magic to keep vengeance at bay. Not even close.

Pulling itself upright, a staff in one hand is raised on high. An instinctive attempt to breathe meets with vine-woven, smoke-ravaged lungs. There is motion, light, and laughter at the edge of the woods. A bright glow emerges from a tall wooden structure.

Some of those voices from a life long lost are very recognizable.

A snarl emerges from somewhere within a withered interior, turning towards the light. It was firelight, yes, but not emerging from the old sentinels. A smirk, a toothy pumpkin mandible, acknowledging the irony of its new facade. A grotesque parody of a Jack-o-lantern, which was the very salvation that would lead it to shrink back into the depths. Yet no guardian gourds to be had.

A host of plump pumpkins lie heaped alongside a shed, freshly picked and harvested. The creature approaches the stock and runs writhing hands over the closest one. Holding the staff aloft, the very same object which had cast it from this world into the next, years prior. There was a sudden burst of heat, a bright flash and the staff returned to its former glory, blazing forth into the autumn night. The torch is lowered into wood, as was seemingly its purpose in this world.The creature steps back, beholding its handiwork, and waits patiently for the fire to cleanse the wicked.

***

The party is in full swing as the night whittles away, closer to the wee hours of November. Bill and Sarah had immaculately decorated the interior of the barn with lavish harvest decorations that evoked a bountiful crop yield and the burgeoning success of a township that was just finding its footing in life.

The pair had stolen away to a private corner of the barn to escape the din, leaving the rest of the adults to celebrate as they saw fit. The schoolmaster, the doctor, and even the reverend were in attendance.

Fermented cider flowed forth and cast a celebratory stupor over the throng. Music played, dancers twirled, food was consumed heartily, and amorous activities became commonplace in the shadow-darkened hay bales. A night of celebration and revelry.

Blinded by gluttony, pride, and lust, wrath itself lingered just outside and made itself known in a burst of heat and flame, before anyone knew what was happening.

"I nearly forgot - will you be taking leave for the evening to tend to your son?" Bill Tassel asks, breathing heavily. The two are huddled into a dark corner, away from the crowd.

Sarah breaks away from his embrace. "He is tucked away in bed. Why should I hasten?"

"Aye", Bill nods. "In the morning, all will see that these superstitions were for naught, including your imaginative boy." They chuckle and move in closer to kiss one another.

Suddenly, the very morning dawn itself seemed to pierce the night. Bill gasps at the sudden intrusion of noise and light, holding Sarah back. The creature stands there, illuminated by fire that eats away a circular penetration in the structure's wood, exposing the barn to the outside world.

The pumpkin-headed figure is all squirming vines, gnarled thorns and smoldering flames. It holds a wheelbarrow with one arm, the contents containing a cluster of pumpkins set aflame. Fire creeps up along the barn and bursts through the window. Bill hears the laughter within suddenly erupt into screams as the building begins to burn.

The creature turns toward him, setting the wheelbarrow down forcefully as embers dance in the air. The other hand clutches Bill's own pitchfork, emitting an eerie glow. It releases a chilling screech, the sound of dead leaves carried on a dry wind. The figure rushes at him with speed far greater than he had expected a dead man ought to run.

Bill feels the sudden puncture in his gut and his body lifts off of the floor. He hears the being speak from somewhere deep within a nightmare landscape of molded pumpkin innards and singed flesh.

"Embrace the flames, so speaketh the Pyrum." Thrusting forward once more, the farmer is pinned to the burning wooden structure as the fire begins to creep towards him. Pyrum steps back to admire the handiwork. Bill remains upright, affixed to the wall with his own implement as life trickles out of him in great gouts of red.

Pyrum reaches out and snaps off a metal prong from the pitchfork with a great show of strength, leaving the rest of the tool to hold the farmer in place. Pressing the metal to Bill's face, reveling in the fear and fire that glinted off of the farmer's tear-soaked eyes, Pyrum chuckles, a deep bellow of sound, and pulls Bill's head upright with a thorn covered-fist, pressing the pitchfork tine to his throat.

"A good harvest this year," the words are uttered, as the life form begins to carve.

Sarah is frozen with fear, helpless and bearing witness to the slaughter. She hears the frightened screams from within as the inferno tears through the party inside.

She tears away from the slaughter and runs blindly into the autumn haze toward the pumpkin patch, but trips almost instantly, her feet entangling upon a thick vine emerging from the fertile soil below. She grasps about, sobbing into the dirt, vision obscured by tears and fog. She pulls herself upright, grasping something round and thick for support.

She thought Bill had already harvested the pumpkins for the year, yet her hands shifted in the murk to another round crop. This one felt smaller, less spherical. A soft, mossy material on top, indentations pressed into the front as though already carved for the season. A sticky sensation, dripping and oozing into her grasp.

Clothing beneath, an old vest and unbuttoned overcoat which she recognized.

Then, a light emerges before her, a candle suddenly lit and dispelling the fog. Sarah lets out a ragged scream as the mutilated head of Bill Tassel lay beneath her blood-encrusted hands. Her lover's head was hollowed out, illuminated from a sallow wick pressed within the viscous interior of the skull. The face was frozen in a frantic scream, eyes and tongue removed to better cast the embers from within.

Sarah screams as a form dressed in Bill's clothes suddenly rises before her. A disembodied wrath to plague the last vestige of All Hallows. Then she sees the pike, a long burning shaft, come towards her. She cringes and closes her eyes, but the sharpened edge bypasses her and instead skewers the occipital bone of the farmer's severed head. As he lifts the staff in the air, he creates a makeshift torch of insanity-lacing fear.

The torch bearer moves the blazing head closer to its own form. The leering face of the indignant creature stares down from atop Bill's attire, now haphazardly draped over a humanoid figure of ivy and soot. The being growls, grabs Sarah by her hair, and pulls her upward, pressing the severed head closer to her, mockingly. She screams as strands are ripped from her scalp from the force of being lifted, and from pure panic.

"I thank thee for the seed," the creature snarls. Sarah finds herself thinking back, her mind racing through the dregs of the past. She remembers the fire, the execution and the agony. She recalls the blood and the pumpkin she had dropped, bursting seeds forth into the carnage soaked-ground before her. She knew then who stood before her, gaping from within the jagged maw of the harvest blight.

"Balthazar Bones," she gasps, choking on sobs. "I am so sorry. We are all sorry."

Pyrum slowly turns his head away from the sniveling woman and toward the flickering barn fire beyond the fog-draped field.

He snorts, a bestial sound, then pulls her off of the ground to make eye contact. Sarah writhes in his grasp as the fetid, rotting gourd fills her nostrils with the scent of old dirt, fresh blood and arcane agony.

"They burn so well," Pyrum observes.

***

Jacob sits upon the wooden porch extending from the Irving cabin. He holds the lit Jack-o-lantern in his lap, being careful not to jostle it. The village is quiet; all of the other children were still asleep. Each dark house a tomb, no lights to be seen, no wards to frighten away the ghouls and beasts that dared to traipse on the edge of All Hallows Eve.

He stands, carrying the lantern with him as he paces throughout the dirt path before him. His mother would be home soon, he imagined, as the party at Farmer Bill's barn seemed to have died down. Once on her way back, he would be able to spot her far down the path and would have the pumpkin long gone before then. He looked forward to returning to his soft, warm bed to doze away the remaining hours of the night. Safe, sound, and protected from harm.

What time is it? It has to be past midnight, surely? His thoughts become distracted by another light in the distance at the edge of the village, just before the road splinters off toward the fields and forest. Curiosity bore upon Jacob as he decided to approach it, still clutching the Jack-o-lantern. More lights, illuminated orbs placed close to the ground. A trail of warmth and light on either side of the path guiding him towards the edge of civilization and into the unknown mists beyond.

He knows he should have turned back then, but a shadowy form at the end of the path holds another light high above, as though suspended in the air. The figure is wearing the same overcoat and vest that Bill Tassel often wore. *Speak of the Devil,* Jacob passes by Bill's Food and Drug on the right of the path, another dark and silent sentinel to add more foreboding to the night.

Farmer Bill will know where mother is, and can guide us back home. He cursed quietly under his breath, uttering a word that would have surely earned a swift beating, had an adult heard the exclamation. *Why have I wandered so far into the fog?* It was a foolish mistake, but Bill could certainly help him.

Jacob passes along the lanterns gleaming from either side of the path and finds himself facing the back of Farmer Bill. The old man smells of

Earth, rot and something sour. *He must have been working the fields earlier, or worked up a sweat at the party.* The figure turns toward the boy, holding an illuminated staff upright. Both individuals recoil in horror at the other.

For Jacob, it was the sight of the pumpkin-headed spook, slathered in ashes and splatters of gore. For the creature himself, it is the sentry ward of the boy's homemade lantern repelling him further away, the accursed glow crisping its pumpkin-flesh upon contact, old magic set upon his form.

Jacob hears the beastly figure hiss in the darkness and he knew then that the legends were true. Monsters born of hatred and blood soaked soil, summoned by the magic of the night to claim vengeance. In all its rotted glory, Pyrum lunges forward, but falls back with another screech as the Jack-o-lantern's light casts upon his body.

Emboldened, Jacob thrusts the pumpkin forward, holding the protection ward out before him. He wants to curl up, hide and pray the beast away, but the boy remains steadfast and never takes his eyes off of the snarling spectre, even as it backs further away.

"Back! Get back!" Jacob yells. Then, a voice calls out through the mist in response, rasping blades on fragile flesh. "Keepeth thee to the lights, boy. Behold my handiwork."

In spite of himself, Jacob obeys and glances at the lights on either side of the path, surrounding him in their gleam. The amber glows spill forth from a litany of severed heads, each one a member of the township. He recognizes the schoolmaster, the minister, the town drunk, every adult in town. Except for one. One that he feared to witness but needed to find.

Hollowed skulls and empty minds, faces carved into gasps of horror and others scoured messily into makeshift grins. They are crude parodies of the very salvation he holds in his hands. Some burned and blackened, others dripping with fresh cuts and newborn gouges in tender flesh.

The shock of it all is too much for the young boy to bear. He screams into the night, dropping the Jack-o-lantern and covering his eyes with his hands. He begins to utter prayers, but he still hears a wet thunk in his near vicinity through his feverish chanting. He pries one eye open between his fingers to see the fresh innards and sputtering candle of his protective lantern spilled from his grasp, smearing the ground and intermingling with the head-lanterns. As arcane blood magic took root in fertile soil, the pumpkin innards began to intertwine with dangling veins and limp tendons. The heads began to twitch and gasp, imbued with life that shouldn't be.

The detached heads let out a collective scream. Horrid shrieks and wordless cries emerging between bruised lips, slashed arteries and jagged clumps of bone. Golden lights befouled by moans of horror pressing in from every side, growing louder and more malignant with each passing second. Jacob closes his eyes and covers his ears, loudly yelling words of the Lord to drown out the horrible sounds.

A thrust of wind spirals through the path, silencing each shriek and extinguishing every candle. Jacob is left alone in the dark with only the sound of his whimpering to keep him company. He feels the looming shadow merge closer to his own. He looks up at the pear shaped shadow above, and Pyrum leans down, kicking aside pumpkin innards derisively.

Sightless eyes stare back through the pumpkin face, specks of blood dotting the orange muscle. "Please, do not hurt me," Jacob whimpers, but not a hint of sympathy comes from old Pyrum.

"The sins of the fathers, little one. Suffer little children to come unto me, and forbid them not: for of such is my kingdom." The child could merely stutter in response, and Pyrum lets out a snort of derision. "No harm will befall thee. I obey the laws of the old world. Thy guardian flame is snuffed, yet it was after the stroke of midnight. One. Minute. Past. Pray that we do not cross paths, and that you keep the fires lit."

The boy nods, tears staining his cheeks and the smell of blood in the air making his nose burn. "Empty promises, for the mischief of children is unquenchable. Still, my vengeance is satisfied. I shall return upon a future harvest. Until then child, take this token to spread thy gospel. Remember the old ways, or embrace the chaos of the flame."

Pyrum places a round object into Jacob's hands, pats his shoulder with a fetid claw and strides past. Had the boy glanced over his shoulder, he would have seen the figure fading into the mist, enshrouded by the depths of autumn's shadows and passing back into the realm of legend.

Jacob stifles a sob and glances around at the carnage surrounding him. The moon overhead is obscured by clouds, blotting out the parade of human remains and strands of pumpkin seeds scattered about. He holds tight to the object in his hands, wishing it would kindle and scare away the shadows once again.

As the clouds part and shine the bane of the harvest moon down upon the massacre, Jacob gets his wish. The round object ignites, a single candle sputtering to life in his grasp. She gazes back at him, chestnut hair falling in ragged clumps and an all-too-familiar face. His mother gazes horridly back at him, her severed head clutched in his trembling grasp.

He drops the head to the ground where it rolls upright, the candle still shining forth. Sarah's features are carved into jagged shards, indicative of a Jack-o-Lantern. He covers his eyes but the damage is done. The amber light of the flame grows in his mind until it obscures everything, leaving only a single flickering image imprinted forever into the corruption of his childhood.

The screaming begins again but this time, it is Jacob who yells hopelessly into the night.

***

October, 1933

The landscape of the world inevitably changes over time. Years pass, seasons come and go, land developed and the days moving by with scarcely a moment to notice. Yet one constant remains in this small town: blood is forever and vengeance never dies. It festers in the dirt, hibernating until the thirst is quenched.

The days grow short, shadows long, while the crops waste and wither. However, the spirit of those who wish to purge the world remains just below our feet.

It is never fully satisfied. So too it would come to pass, one All Hallow's Eve night over two centuries later, that the magic of the harvest season would contaminate the ground once more.

During his time underground, Pyrum had maintained a semblance of lucidity. The Earth above had churned and rolled with age, the footsteps of time flowing past. Yet he was still there, slumbering on the edge of the Western Woods, sleeping with satisfaction until one day, the soil grew loose around his form.

Balthazar Bones had long been eclipsed by the ravages of flame and so, on this night, Pyrum rises again. Twitching vines whip at the fresh air and the pumpkin visage of the creature presses forth from beneath the ground. He stands, shaking the loose dirt off of form-fitting clothes, hefting a staff into the air.

With a hint of delight, he notes that the head of the old farmer perched upon its staff was now overgrown with smaller vines, contorted into the resemblance of a miniature pumpkin. A fitting accoutrement.

Pyrum looks around at new settings. The Western Woods have grown considerably smaller. Beyond the tree line, wizened eyes spy a familiar collection of buildings. He is surprised that the village would still be standing. Beyond this, there is a bustle of activity in Boggy Meadow that must be investigated.

He presses forward, dirt shaking off of its form, adjusting the vest and straining at the stiffness of ages left to immobility. He comes upon an open gate, and takes in the sight before his eyes. The pumpkin patch is long gone, razed into flat land. Several buildings surround the perimeter, aglow with light. He sniffs at the air, olfactory senses long erased, yet an intangible sense emerges from within his maw.

By some miracle, he can feel the chill of the harvest season, sense the crisp air whipping about lightly in the cool night. The amber moon shines from above and casts light on a new domain.

He sees Jack-o-lanterns scattered about, which upon first reflexes causes a tensing up of the beast's shoulders, snapping his eyes shut. When he does not feel the searing pain of their glow, upon further inspection, they appear to be decorational. Not made of Earth and fire. There is joy, celebration, dancing, and music -

not from the origins of gluttony or sin, rather born from brotherhood and tragedy.

Stepping forth from around a statue, a gaunt figure sports a smart suit, cane and a jaunty top hat. As it moves closer, Pyrum cannot detect any wisp of living humanity, or flesh to carve. This being is something else.

Pyrum stands his ground, vines writhing and staff clutched tight as the figure stops before him. A gnarled hand composed almost entirely of bone is outstretched for a handshake. Pyrum grunts in surprise, smirking at the sight of a grinning skull peering from beneath the brim of the hat.

"Well, hello there, friend," the phantom speaks, a masculine voice as smooth as a farmer's spade. "Would thou tell me, what is this place? I have been away for many a year." Pyrum asks. "It's your new home, if you so choose. I feel you would be well suited here."

Pyrum gazes among the courtyard and sees a collection of other figures approaching. Though mortal, he could sense that these were beings of legend, shadow, blood, and myth.

Excited, he happily takes the limpid bones of this new benefactor into his own dirt-slathered grip. A supernatural handshake as new friends cheer in the background.

The skeletal man grins wider and holds out his cane. Pyrum's staff taps against it, and the vine-entangled head atop begins to glow as bright as the harvest moon. With this union, the light eclipses everything beyond the fringes of legend and lore.

CHAPTER 7
Darla

Early Winter, 1933

A small child is huddled in a cave to try and seek refuge from the cold. She wraps her arms around herself, but still shudders violently from the wind that seeps in. She gazes toward the entrance of the cave at the lifeless body of a full grown bear.

Tears form in her eyes. The demise of this majestic beast was her fault, she was sure of it. This cave, the bear and her small batch of cubs was all this child could remember. She knew she was different from her surrogate family, as she would regard herself in the reflection of the creek water next to them and note their disparities. However, they made her part of their sleuth and now, that bond has been shattered.

Hours earlier, maybe even days ago, another human attacked their lair. A male. The trauma of the event made the details a blur. All she allowed herself to remember was the mother bear fighting the hunter, her cubs running away during the onslaught, and a loud boom followed by stark silence.

She tried earlier to pull the carcass into the cave with no success. The idea was to use it to protect against the frigid air that made its way into her dwelling, at least until the sun was up or the unforgiving wind was gone. The creature however was much too heavy, and the child was too weak from hunger and exhaustion.

She turns her view to a corner of the cave, where another corpse resides. Earlier, she searched the woods for the cubs who ran off in the melee of the attack, but was only able to find one. It was not a happy reunion.

Her little brother bear was attacked by a larger animal, likely a wolf, which left behind a ghastly scene. Bite marks, dried blood, and the face torn off to reveal the skull underneath. She scooped the cub in her arms and brought him back to the cave to be with his mother once more. As best of an impromptu funeral a child could endeavor.

The little girl finally succumbs to her sadness and cries in sorrow. The tears that roll down her cheeks start to freeze. The high altitude makes the temperature drop faster than the world below. Her stomach growls and as if a sign of mercy from the heavens, the smell of food wafts in the air.

She tries to place the scent. Her bear family had consumed human food a few times before, as they scoured trash left behind at camping sites when they knew the coast was clear. It has a sweet smell. As the tantalizing scent drifts inside the cave, the far away sounds of music, laughter and screams also make their way up the mountain.

Something compels her to pursue these sounds and smells. She stands to begin her departure from the cave, but turns to regard her little brother. Her lip quivers, and she picks him up, carrying him lovingly as if he were still alive and needed protection.

As she leaves the cave, she stops and walks over to the mother bear's corpse. She ignores the open wound where the gunshot blast is located, and instead focuses on the creature's face, now still and motionless. As more tears escape, she places a gentle kiss on the momma bear's forehead, then departs the safety of the cave.

***

Sir Henry looks upon his fairgrounds with delight. If he could smile, he would, but he welcomes the internal feeling of joy. It had been a long time since he felt like this.

Screams of delight and music swell all around. He regards the young Poppy, wearing a decorative mask and merrily chasing around a group of children with her large, novelty scissors. "Momma always said, don't run with scissors," she yells at them playfully.

He also catches sight of Vex, who is currently sneaking up behind a group enjoying cotton candy. She brings her staff close to the shoulder of the largest member of the group, and lets a small spark fly out of the spokes. She yells "boo!" and the combined loud noises cause the group of people to collectively jump. They yelp, and then laugh in relief when the scare is over, hands to chests or covering their mouths as they giggle nervously.

All of the sights, sounds and fragrances were intoxicating. It truly felt alive here again. He wishes that Mr. Barloc could be here to see this, but he was subdued by a mountain of paperwork with investors, according to his most recent correspondence. Nevertheless, the finances of Sir Henry's operations were secure and their vision was realized in a way they did not anticipate.They even expected to make a profit by 1934.

Sir Henry feels eyes on him, and he turns his gaze to the entrance of the grounds to see a small child. He can't explain it, but something is not right. There is an unease to her presence. He grabs his cane and hobbles forward to further investigate. As he draws closer, he is taken aback by what he sees.

This little girl is filthy, with limp black hair that settles upon tattered clothing, outgrown long ago, and definitely ill suited for the cold weather. She grips what looks like a teddy bear, but she also has what appears to be a severely cleft lip. She is malnourished and has dark circles under her eyes.

Without a word spoken between them, Sir Henry knew this was an abandoned child. He was aware of how cruel the world was to those who were different, whether it was in physical appearance or how you veered from the norm. Especially after the revelation he had earlier this year, he could not even begin to imagine the hardships this young girl has endured. Yet somehow, she found her way here.

He holds out his bony hand, causing her to jump slightly, and she grips her fuzzy companion tighter. "Come along, dear child, you're safe here." She studies his hand, and looks up into the kindness of his eyes. Though she does not fully understand, she grabs his palm, and is ushered inside to her new home.

As they walk hand in hand into the fairgrounds, snow begins to fall.

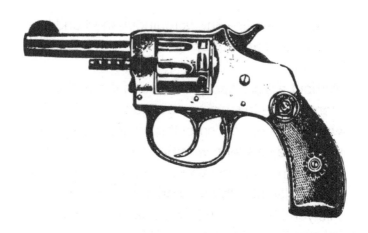

CHAPTER 8
The Boogeyman

Late Winter, 1933

A jarring cold grips the land. Significant snow fell once this season, but lately, only a slight dusting has been seen on the ground. Despite the temperatures, people still come to Sir Henry's, so the merry band of eccentrics decided to change the atmosphere to something more cheerful. More festive.

Poppy and Vex had wandered into the woods and chopped down a mid-sized tree, while Kane went with the girls to help carry it back. All together, this newfound family decorated it with popcorn strung along a puppet's thread, pinecones painted with lightning bolt silver, and a star made from crinkled yet shiny red candy wrappers. Everyone has swapped scares for cheer, wearing festive garb, while Sir Henry makes himself scarce, working behind the scenes. *Skeletons do not fit the tone of the season*, he shared with the group.

Once the clock chimes 9PM, the delighted tourists exit the fairgrounds and make their way home, likely to families to celebrate the joys this winter season brings. Sir Henry feels less than jovial, despite his best efforts. He sits in his study, putting aside the latest letter from Mr. Barloc, and retrieves a framed photo in his bony hands as kindling crackles in his fireplace, expelling warmth.

He looks upon a photo of his Bride. Since he was laying dormant in a grave for a few years, this would officially be his first Christmas without her. The grief and nostalgia created an awful gnawing in his heart. Though he was happy to not be alone, it made him feel empty to look at the lovely decorations that his new friends had placed across the property. He just prayed he would feel differently on the actual day that Christmas occurred, or that he could put on a brave act for the others.

His quiet pondering is broken by a loud commotion outside, broken glass and screaming. He bolts out of his chair and tosses on a coat. "Poppy! Vex?!" He yells out for someone to answer him as he exits his house.

He feels a sickening deja vu as he sees a small fire licking the side of the quarters of the performer's home. It is not as horrible as that dreadful night years before, but it triggers awful memories that fill his heart with dread.

He snaps himself out of it and quickly evaluates the scene, yelling instructions. "Poppy, grab the fire extinguisher from the shed! Vex and Kane, do your best to shovel dirt into the fire to extinguish it. Did anyone see what happened?" As his team flies into action, he sees Darla huddling in a corner, shaking, holding her brother bear tight. "What did you see, sweetheart? What happened?"

Though they had been working for weeks to try and teach her how to speak, the efforts were very slow. She was able to lift one shaky hand and point towards the Western Woods.

As if on some sort of sick queue, a loud shot rings out in the night. A bullet hits the ground near Sir Henry's feet, sending up shards of dirt, dead grass and snow into the air. Screams echo at the noise, and Sir Henry spots the culprit. A dark figure stands at the edge of the trees, a smoking gun in the right hand. The assailant just stands there, slowly lowering his arm, eyes glinting as he stares.

Sir Henry huffs in anger and turns back to Darla. "You stay here with the others. This ends tonight." He stalks toward the figure, shaking with rage as he draws closer.

The stranger takes off and darts into the forest, but not far behind, the protagonist closely pursues the villain. Luckily, due to the extensive development of the land, there is a shortage of woodland to wander through. Sir Henry is quickly able to corner this terrorist in a bare patch of land, a barbed wire fence with wooden posts marking the territory of a neighboring farm behind them.

"It was you, wasn't it? You set that fire years ago, and you tried to do it again. Who are you and what do you want?" The stranger keeps his back to him. "Talk, coward!"

He is met with an evil chuckle. "Now, is that any way to talk to your brother?"

He turns and reveals his face to Sir Henry. He wears a dark, black cloak. His brown hair is dirty, overgrown and tousled. A scar on his cheek looks very familiar. The antagonist's corroded teeth peer out from his arrogant smirk, his breath hanging in the cold air. He reaches into his cloak, then flings an item in Sir Henry's direction. He cautiously regards the stranger, kneeling down to pick up an old family photograph. Crinkled and faded. The very same one which tormented him months prior. A sudden flood of horrible realization dawns on him.

"It is you," Sir Henry states, his voice small with confusion and emotion. "It's true?"

The other man nods and his thumb strokes the hammer of his revolver, nestled in a holster around his waist. "Not quite the reunion you wanted?"

Sir Henry grounds himself back to reality. "What is your name?" The other man shrugs. "Does it matter?"

"Of course it does." A scoff in return. "Many of them, including the latest one I got to, call me The Boogeyman. She was screaming it right before I put the trigger in between her eyes," he stated with a vile timbre of sick pride. "The way the blood splattered on the wall behind her. The fear. Just, so satisfying. One click of a little metal toggle, and then-"

"Enough!" Sir Henry bellows into the night, cutting off his evil monologue. "Tell me why? Why are you hurting people? Why have you come after me?"

The morbid outlaw regards Sir Henry, tilting his head. "Boy, you sure look repulsive. How are you even alive anyway?" When the skeleton figure does not satisfy his cruel question with a response, the other man decides to answer the previous set of questions.

"They never meant to have you. But even though you were the mistake, they found some new program where they could get some nice cash for selling off a healthy baby to a well-to-do family," the sinner revealed. "They tried to do the same with me, but I was just too damn old and ugly for anyone to give a damn about, I guess. So good ol' ma and pa worked my fingers to the bone with their business, from as young as five years old."

Sir Henry crossed his arms. "What did they do?"

"Do you really care?"

"Why would I ask if I did not want an answer?"

A sigh. "Butchers. That was no place for a boy to grow up in, but that's also where I got my first taste. How I got so good at it."

The other man starts to slowly skulk towards Sir Henry, his thumbs hooked around his belt loops in a cocky manner. "You see, they had me using a captive bolt for killing the pigs and the cows. They considered it easy work for me," This man reeks of sweat, his clothes filthy. Tokens of years on the run in the shadows. "The problem is, I grew to love it. The look in the animal's eyes, the light being extinguished when I pulled the trigger."

He steps very close to Sir Henry, testing his patience. "The only thing more satisfying was when I used that same damn tool on my old man. I purposely woke him up so he would realize what was happening, and boy, did it please me to see his pupils dilate. The trickle of blood rolling down his stupid face."

"You killed our father?" Sir Henry asks this question, horror in his voice.

A mean laugh is his answer. "Nothing gets past you, does it? I also killed Ma, but I smothered her with a pillow. I just wanted to see how long it would take. I found that I prefer more instant gratification. When I finally shut them up and was free of their servitude, I was able to find his gun in the closet," he says, pulling the gun out of the holster and regarding it with a macabre reverence.

"There are other times, where I have experimented with other methods," he continues, acid in his voice. "Especially when I wanted to stamp out your picturesque situation. Oh, how I searched for you, brother. To find that you got this pretty little life was just so," he cackles, not able to finish his sentence. "Just so unfair! So you see, I had to make it more personal. Oh, yes."

"You killed her, didn't you?" Sir Henry asks, afraid to know the answer but already aware in his heart. His voice is choked with tears of sorrow and rage.

"Of course. After I broke into a military base for more ammo, I was also able to find their infirmary. I grabbed two nice hypodermic needles and arsenic. Way more than the human body can handle. Especially for someone of her size." Sir Henry grits his teeth as tears make their way down his face, the torture of the truth cutting to his soul.

"So dainty, she was. Make no mistake, she fought me though. She struggled so much I could not look her in the eyes, like I normally get to, but when I slid both needles in her pale flesh and injected her, it was enough satisfaction knowing what I took from you. When she went limp, I wiped the froth from her mouth and took my leave."

Sir Henry chokes back a sob. "And the fire?" He asks this question, his voice faltering despite his best efforts to stabilize his voice.

"To purify the Earth of that band of freaks you had, of course. You see, I know I am not right in the head, brother. There are too many misfits and weirdos and orphans wandering this planet, suffering," he shares. "I end their tribulations, yet you mock them, oddities on full display for the price of admission."

The cloaked figure lifts the gun to Sir Henry, a mischievous smile creasing his face. "Once I am done with you, I'll go back and finish the job with the rest of those abnormalities you have back there." With that statement, he charges at Sir Henry, grunting with exertion. With an ungodly strength, fueled by fury and sorrow, Sir Henry wraps his arms around the other man's midsection and forces him to the ground. He is able to wrangle the gun out of his hand and points it at him, his mangled hair spread out on the ground.

"Go ahead and shoot me," the villain utters, hate shining in his eyes. Sir Henry lets his finger slightly brush the trigger, reaching back to cock the gun. But the Witch's words dance around in his mind. He instead points the gun upright, empties the chamber, spilling the bullets to the ground, and tosses the gun far over the fence, into the neighboring field.

"Though you deserve it, more than words can say, I will not take your life," Sir Henry states, grunting with effort to keep the other man to the ground. He wrenches his hands into the fabric of his dirty cloak, looking him intensely in the eyes. "You will never again set foot on my land. I will turn my back on you and never think of you another day further, despite the atrocities you have shared with me today."

Tears continue to stream down his face, hitting the snow covered ground beneath him. "I forgive you. You're a sick man who had a hard life. You needed help and compassion. It does not justify what you have done, but it is not for me to decide how your story ends." He forcefully lets go of the man, knocking him back into the ground, snow and dirt dispersing under his weight. Sir Henry starts walking away from the scene, but of course, inferior people always need to have the last word.

"Awfully arrogant of you to say I won't come back!" Sir Henry turns to regard the heartless man, still sitting on the ground. "I know where you live! You may pretend to have honor, but I certainly don't. What makes you think I won't stop until I've ended you?!"

Sir Henry takes in a faltering breath. "Because I have friends who will do the things I have no stomach for."

The ground quakes as a form slowly rises behind the other man. A large figure stomps forward, the barbed wire fence topping over as he takes a massive step. The spiked metal tears at his form, but it does little to stop him.

The sinner turns. An immense creature with a gourd shaped head looms over him. He grips an ominous staff, and takes in a deep breath, closing his eyes. As the being lets out a satisfied sigh, the noise causes the ground to rumble beneath them both.

"You carry with you the stench of injustice," the beast utters, a hungry tone to his voice. "It is intoxicating." The murderer shudders. "Who-what are you?" No sooner had he asked that question did the creature sink his claws around his midsection, puncturing the sharp ends of his vine-like hands into the mortal's ribs, belly and hips. He yells out in agony as the ominous being wrenches him up to meet him at eye level.

"I am Pyrum," he growled. "And thou will never harm another soul again." With that, he cracks open his monstrous gob, his carved pumpkin jaws forming serrated, rotted teeth. As the killer screams in pain and terror, he is shoveled face first into the mouth of the beast.

Pyrum chomps down, biting through flesh, the liver, spleen, and tissue. He bites at the spine, with the same sound and fervor as snapping a wishbone in two, until the lower body falls to the ground below. His evil blood stains the dusting of snow on the ground, and his legs twitch with the last remnants of life.

The being shuts his eyes and makes a noise of delight as he slowly consumes his prey. His pre-hibernation meal, as he will retreat into the bloody soil once finished.

In the distance, a man with a skeleton visage begins the journey home, hopeful that his colleagues were able to put out the fire. All the while, a black cat with silver eyes watches the scene, anger billowing under her ancient fur.

EPILOGUE
Jack Frost

The cold embrace of dark. The blinding luminosity of winter's twilight sun, darting through the trees and reflecting off the snow, is long gone.

The life among the forest, who make their homes in the trees and burrow in the ground, sleep soundly. Icicles hang from branches as snow gently falls from the sky.

Footsteps in the snow begin to approach. The stars above the trees glow just a bit brighter. Here we find the joyous Jack Frost, a light blue glow emanating from his flesh as he traverses the ground.

Wearing a debonair blue suit, ice crystals glittering on his shoulders, he looks out of place trudging snow that is ankle deep in an empty forest. Yet his existence personifies jubilation, and the cold does little to harm him.

Jack was on his way back home to Winter Ville to his stately mansion, the Ice Palace. He hoped to make it through this holiday season without a run-in with the evil South Pole Elf, but that's a story perhaps for another time.

Something was different about this night. This year, in fact, was different. Much loss. It seemed like the nights were darker, as well. The terrain was foreign compared to past wintertide migrations, and Jack feared he was lost.

"Okay, calm down, old boy," Jack whispered to himself. "Just look for that Northern Star, and it will be fine. You'll be home soon."

Frost looked to the sky, holding up his hand and emitting a glow so he could better see the stars. Alas, no luck. He lowered both his hands to his head to look ahead of him on the trail. What he saw drained the bright blue color of his skin to white in terror.

A man walked towards him, between the trees that seemed to bow to his frightful presence, dressed in as equally a spruce manner as Jack. Yet this man, this being, was the polar opposite.

A black tux with traces of dirt. A black top hat with a shiny purple accent. A cane. A faint smell of blood drifts in the cold evening air.

"E-excuse me, sir?" Jack called out. "You sure look like you know your way around these woods. Might I ask for assist-"

Jack's words, like his sense of direction this dark night, became lost. This man was practically a walking skeleton. Despite his state of decomposition, his eyes still looked alive. He blinked a few times, hoping his mind was playing tricks on him, but the man was there before him.

"How might I be of service?" His voice was croaky, higher in pitch, tired. Despite his shocking appearance, his spirit still exuded a warm tone of generosity, hospitality.

"Well, I uh, I was looking for Winter Ville. It's North of here." Sir Henry nodded. He turned and pointed his cane to a path that snaked through a patch of snow-covered pine trees. "T-thank you. How far would you say?" The dark figure stepped closer to Jack, and answered. "Perhaps an hour."

Jack shuddered, as they were inches apart. "I pray you are not going to do harm to me, good sir?"

The gaunt figure reaches forward with a bony hand, and Jack winces. He feels the ghoul straighten his pristine white bowtie, so he opens his eyes. The way the shadow of the moon plays on the stranger's ghastly face, it almost looks like a smile. Jack's pale eyes, surrounded by a royal blue skin tone, meet the stranger's gaze.

"Why would I do that?" He states with a playful tone to his voice. "After all, it's Christmas time."

With that, Sir Henry makes his way further down the trail and deeper into the woods, leaving behind a confused and shaken Jack Frost.

Perhaps tomorrow he will find more beings left behind by society, more outcasts to add to his family.

For now, for this rare peaceful moment, this night walk was just for him.

THE STORIES AS VERSES

PROLOGUE - Jeremiah 29:11

CHAPTER 1 - Isaiah 41:10

CHAPTER 2 - Ephesians 2: 4-5

CHAPTER 3 - John 8:12

CHAPTER 4 - 2 Corinthians 5:17

CHAPTER 5 - Psalm 16:11

CHAPTER 6 - Mark 9:37

CHAPTER 7 - Matthew 7: 1-5

CHAPTER 8 - Psalm 86:5

EPILOGUE - Jeremiah 6:16

Beatrice

Pyrum

Darla

Made in the USA
Las Vegas, NV
16 December 2024

14325810R00085